Lyla Lyte
and the
Loot Tree

Other books by I'deyah Ricketts

Lyla Lyte and the Li'berry Fruit

Where Are the Animals?
(Children's Picture Book)

For more information about the author, visit
ideyahricketts.com.

Lyla Lyte
and the
Loot Tree

by I'deyah Ricketts

illustrated by Katie Williams

Climbing Clouds Publishing
Chicago

I dedicate this book to my family...
I love you all.

Contents

1
The New Library

"I'm finally done!," Lyla Lyte exclaimed as she jumped up from where she was sitting on her bed, legs crisscrossed, and heaved a sigh of relief. She had just completed her poetry masterpiece, which had taken a three-hour brain workout. Crumpled notebook papers, pencil stubs, and worn out erasers were flung across her room. A Maya Angelou poetry book lay face down on her orange-with-blue-polka-dots comforter, which was strewn across her bed.

"Whoaaa!" Lyla said, looking inside her notebook. "I never knew poetry was so difficult to write!"

She stepped in front of her tall dresser-mirror and started reading each stanza aloud, like she was performing in a poetry recital.

Afterward, a confident smile lit up her small, round face. She gave herself a thumbs-up. She felt like her experiment with poetry was a complete success. "I didn't know I had it in me," she said, boastful and a tad bit cocky. "I guess *I'm* a little Ms. Maya Angelou in the making. Maybe I'll write a poetry book someday."

"Lyla, make sure you clean your room," Mrs.

Lyte called out from downstairs, interrupting Lyla's daydream about being a famous poet.

"OK, I will," Lyla hollered back. "Now, what should I call my poem?" She thought hard, but nothing came to mind, so she surveyed her room, looking for anything that would spark an idea. Stacks of books dotted the carpeted floor. Her small, wood bookshelf had reached its limit, and the carpet was the next most popular choice. On top of one of the piles was a chapter book called *Stink and the World's Worst Super Stinky Sneakers*. Because it took Lyla only one hour to read one hundred and thirty-six pages, it was a record-breaking book. She purposely sat it on top of the pile to showcase it like a trophy.

Suddenly, Lyla's eyes opened wider accompanied by her *O* shaped mouth. "I got it! I know what it should be!" Lyla penciled in the title at the top of the notebook paper. "It's perfect!"

She scanned her poem one final time for good measure, checking for any misspelled words. Then she shut her notebook and shot down the stairs like a speeding bullet, nearly tripping over the last step.

Lyla burst into the kitchen, wanting to surprise her mom with her newfound talent. "Mom look!" she shouted, thrilled.

"Did you clean your room yet?" asked her mom with her back to Lyla. Mrs. Lyte, wearing her green flowery oven mitts, was removing a baking pan of jerk chicken from the oven. She was preparing dinner, which also consisted of whipped mashed potatoes and broccoli.

"Ummm...I'm halfway to finishing, but guess what I wrote!" Lyla responded, suddenly anxious. Without giving her mom time to reply, she answered her own question. "It's a poem for Mayor Crinkle, thanking him for agreeing to build the new library." She opened her notebook to the page with her poem and held it out. "Read it!"

"Now, you know I can't read while I'm cooking," Mrs. Lyte said as she placed the steaming hot dish of chicken on the stovetop. "And since when did you start writing poetry?"

"I've been reading a book of poems written by the great poet Maya Angelou," Lyla replied, hugging the notebook against her chest. "I thought that since Mayor Crinkle changed for the better and is doing so much for us I could write a wonderful poem showing him how much we appreciate it. And you know how much I *love* to write."

"I think that's a splendid idea!" her mom said, turning off the oven. "Just read it out loud to me."

"OK," Lyla said as she enthusiastically reopened her notebook. "But you have to give me your undivided attention."

Mrs. Lyte turned to face Lyla, took off her oven mitts, and laid them down on the granite counter top. "I'm all ears."

"Here it goes," Lyla cleared her throat and read the title first, "Mayor Crinkle Is Not a Stinkle." She peeked over the top of her notebook to see her mom's reaction. Mrs. Lyte restrained herself from laughing and gave Lyla an encouraging smile. Lyla returned the smile and continued.

When Lyla was finished reading, her mom was unable to hold it in any longer. She chuckled and told her daughter, "Great job! I think the mayor is going to absolutely *love* it."

Mayor Crinkle Is Not a Stinkle!

I just wanted to say thanks for everything.

I'm sorry if I told you that you could not sing.

At first, I thought you were a terrible brute,

Until the day you read your own Li'berry Fruit.

And that day, under the tree you changed.

To our surprise you gave the town a new name.

So thank you for the town's new library.

Where we can read about mysteries, fairytales,

and stories that are extremely scary.

Now children in Coverfield will be great readers forever.

Mayor Crinkle...you're the best mayor ever!

"Can you take me to City Hall to give it to him after school tomorrow?" Lyla asked.

Lyla's mom turned her attention to the refrigerator. She opened the door and took out a forest of broccoli from the bottom vegetable tray. "You can ask your dad when he comes home."

"Awww, broccoli for dinner!" Lyla stared at the handful of miniature trees as her mom walked over to the sink to give them a quick bath before filling a small pot with water and placing it on the hot stove. "Why do we have to eat vegetables every night?" she asked, squishing up her face.

"Because it's a good source of vitamins for your body," replied Mrs. Lyte, sounding like a dietician. "Anyway, this is your brother's favorite vegetable."

Lyla pointed to Dentapotamus restlessly sitting in his baby blue high chair. "If he can eat his boogers, he can eat anything."

Mrs. Lyte ignored Lyla's comment. "Dinner is almost ready young lady, so go wash your hands and set the table," she instructed, placing the freshly bathed broccoli in the boiling water.

"OK," Lyla said. She groaned and turned to walk away.

"Honey, I'm home!" Mr. Lyte called out as he stepped through the front door, wearing black work pants and a short-sleeved, soiled gray shirt with his first name stitched on the left chest. The oil crammed underneath his finger nails showed that he had been working hard all day fixing cars. Lyte's Car Repair had its grand opening six months before, and business had been booming. In one hand he held the house keys, and in the other hand he held a folded copy of that day's Coverfield Gazette, with coffee stains all over it. His morning ritual was reading the newspaper and drinking a cup of freshly brewed coffee before he began his job of auto repair.

Lyla detoured from her route to the bathroom, sprinted to her dad, and wrapped him up with a huge welcome-home hug. "Hi, Dad!" she said. After this daily hug, Lyla would smell like the auto oil that followed Mr. Lyte like cologne.

At the sound of Mr. Lyte's voice, Dentapotomas became antsy and began squirming like a worm trying to escape a fisherman's hook.

"How's my little princess?" Lyla's dad asked.

"I'm great," she answered, brimming with excitement. "I have something to show you." She tugged on her dad's arm to lead him into the living room where she intended him to sit and be a one-person audience.

"Wait, wait…I have something to show you all as well," said her dad, bringing a halt to Lyla's pulling. He tossed his keys on the small table in the foyer but held on to the Coverfield Gazette as he entered the kitchen.

Lyla trailed her dad. "What is it? Is it a gift for one of us?" she asked impatiently.

"Daddy," cried Dentapotamus, frantically trying to escape from the grip of his high chair.

"Hey there, my little man," Mr. Lyte put the newspaper on the island countertop and picked up Dentapotamus, releasing him from his high chair. He bobbed Dentapotamus up and down on his shoulder.

"How was work?" Mrs. Lyte asked, as she put

the cover on the pot of broccoli.

"Busy, as usual," Mr. Lyte replied with a tired smile.

"What did you want to show us?" Lyla asked again.

Her dad recovered his thoughts. Still holding Dentapotamus, he flattened the Coverfield Gazette and turned to page six. "Read this honey," he said to his wife. "'Dog Trained to Read a Book.'" Mrs. Lyte read the first headline that caught her eyes. "That's amazing!"

"That's the wrong one," Mr. Lyte interrupted. He hastily pointed to the article next to it and left a greased dot. "This is the one I want you to read."

Mrs. Lyte looked at the other heading, reading it quickly and silently. She looked at Lyla with worried eyes then turned her attention back to the newspaper. "'No Money to Build the New Library!'" she read.

"Oh no!" Lyla cried. It was a huge disappointment. She couldn't believe what she had just heard. She grabbed the paper and read the article for confirmation. She became more disturbed with *every* word she read. Her expression was a mixture of anger, sadness, and doubt. "This can't be happening!" she said. "Mayor Crinkle promised that he would build Coverfield a new library!"

Just as Mr. Lyte was consoling Lyla with a one-arm hug, Crinkle News Watch aired on their tubevision in the living room. Across the screen in huge red capital letters scrolled, "Special News Report." Mayor Crinkle appeared, standing in a vacant dirt-filled lot wearing his usual purple eyeglasses, red striped suit, and polished black shoes. He removed a bright red handkerchief from his suit pocket and wiped the dripping sweat from his shiny forehead. The camera zoomed in closer allowing just his head to fill the tubevision screen.

"Turn it up," Lyla's mom instructed, watching the tubevision from inside the kitchen.

Lyla released herself from her dad's hug and scrambled to the tubevision. She twisted the knob at the top, cranking up the volume. Mr. Lyte carried Dentapotomus into the living room with Mrs. Lyte trailing behind.

"People of Coverfield, this is a special news report," Mayor Crinkle began, looking tense. "I know everyone is waiting patiently for us to start building Coverfield's new library. I thank all of you, but with a disappointed heart I bring you this news." He took a deep breath. "Due to the city's budget *deficit*, our plans to construct our new library are on hold."

Lyla pulled out the dictionary that she carried around all the time in her right-hand pocket and looked up the word deficit. "Got it!" she declared. "The amount by which a sum of money falls short," she muttered to herself. "This is sooo not good!"

The news camerawoman, Ms. Weatherspoon, zoomed out from Mayor Crinkle and showed the full view of the site where the new library was supposed to be built. In the background, there was a tower of books that looked like the Leaning Tower of Pisa.

"We are short a lot of money," Mayor Crinkle explained. He walked over to a line graph chart drawn on a huge 25" × 30" white flip chart pad sitting on a black easel. "As you all can see." He picked up a foot-long pointer stick that was leaning against the easel and directed the viewers' attention to the graph. The line on the graph started off going up but then shot down toward the bottom. "Over the past five years, the city has been dropping deeper and deeper into a financial hole. It will cost the town a million dollars to build the library. For this reason we will not be able to build it." A sullen expression came over the mayor's face. "As we are having a

new election this year for mayor of Coverfield, I promise you all that finding money to build the new library will be my top campaign priority. Once again, I'm sorry to be reporting this today."

"No one's feeling sorrier than me," Lyla said. She let out a dreadful sigh and plopped herself down on the carpet. A waterfall of tears flowed from her eyes.

With Dentapotomus still in his arms, her dad tilted his head downward and said, "Don't worry princess, we'll get *our* library somehow."

"Yeah, but how?" Lyla asked.

"Where there's a will there's a way," Mr. Lyte reassured her, handing Dentapotamus off to his wife. He took a seat next to Lyla on the plush beige carpet.

Lyla was confused. "What does that even mean?" she asked.

"It means, don't give up hope," he began to explain, wiping away the last tears on her cheeks. "As long as you have that creative mind of yours, you will find a way to help the mayor."

"The only way I would be able to help would

be if I was a millionaire," said Lyla. "Then I would be rich, and I could give him the money the town needs."

Lyla's dad reached into his pants pocket and pulled out his black leather wallet. He took out a few pressed dollar bills. "It's good to have a dream of being rich," he said, waving the dollars bills in front of Lyla. "But sometimes having a lot of money and donating it is not that simple."

"Donate," Lyla repeated the word, unsure of its meaning.

"To give," Mr. Lyte said.

"Having a lot of money can solve any problem," Lyla contradicted her dad. "You can do anything you want to do, and you can share or donate money with everyone."

Mr. Lyte gave Lyla a look and said, "When people know you have a lot of money they tend to act a little crazy!"

"Crazy?" Lyla raised her eyes.

"That's why they say money is the root of all evil." His lecture over, Mr. Lyte placed his money back in its home.

Lyla didn't understand the quote, and she absolutely didn't agree with the idea that money didn't fix the world's problems. But she was encouraged to try to find a way to get the new library.

"OK, Dad," she said, to stop him from delivering more quotes that didn't make any sense.

2

The Science Lesson

Lyla was quiet the whole ride to Crinkle Academy as her mind was stuck on trying to come up with solutions. Last night she couldn't sleep, thinking about not having the library built. It felt like she had slept on a roller coaster. She had never tossed and turned so much in her entire life. In the family van, Mr. Lyte tried to assure Lyla that everything would be OK—that she had nothing to worry about—but she knew that was all a part of a parent's job description: Must be able to make your child feel better.

When they arrived at school, Mr. Lyte planted a kiss on her forehead as she got out of the van.

He drove off slowly, watching her walk sluggishly up to the double doors. She went on into room 201 with her face hung down and her bottom lip poking out.

"I guess you saw the news last night," Lyla's Troops said in unison when they saw her. Lyla raised her head and said in a cracked voice, "It's horrible!"

"I know," said Nick. "The mayor is not building the library because of the *defecate*."

"The word is deficit," Lyla said, correcting him. She pulled out her trusty pocket dictionary and looked up the word Nick had just used. "The word you're using means you have to go to the bathroom and do a number two."

"Ewww!" Samantha and Megan exclaimed, pinching their noses and wrinkling their faces. "That's gross!"

"Don't you think I know that?" Nick said angrily, staring at them all. "I just wanted to make sure you all were paying attention to me when I talk."

Lyla was too worried to get into a

pronunciation duel with Nick. Even though she knew Nick was too embarrassed to admit he was *one hundred percent* wrong, she raised her white flag and surrendered for the very first time, since they had been best friends. "What are we going to do?" she asked. That was her immediate concern.

The Troops couldn't reply because Ms. Verdak had come into the classroom and instructed the class to take their seats so she could take attendance.

Teaching used to be done from tubevisions, but not anymore. Mayor Crinkle had relinquished his position as the tube teacher and chose the Classroom Tube Assistants (CTAs) to be the permanent classroom teachers. Ms. Verdak was assigned to her same room, room 201. When the class had found out the great news, everyone had jumped for joy.

After all the students in the class were accounted for, Ms. Verdak closed her attendance book and laid it on top of her dark brown desk. She turned toward the huge whiteboard and started drawing with blue and red dry-erase markers. When she finished, the class was staring at two overlapping, squiggly lines.

"What's that?" Johnny shouted from the back of the classroom. He strained his eyes to make sense of the confusing image, but it made no difference.

"Someone didn't raise his hand," Ms. Verdak said, still facing the whiteboard.

With a grunt, Johnny raised his hand up high and called Ms. Verdak's name.

"Yes, Johnny," Ms. Verdak said, turning around.

"What is that?" he asked for the second time, eager to get an answer.

"It is part of the science lesson,'" she said. "This morning we will be learning about DNA."

"D-N-A," repeated the class.

Ms. Verdak dove right into the lesson. "Do any of you know why you look different from each other?" she asked, pointing at them.

"You mean why I'm handsome and everyone else is ugly?" Nick said. He was the only one who snickered at his sarcastic response.

Ms. Verdak gave Nick a look that could slice through thin air. "Anyone else?"

No one raised their hands.

Ms. Verdak pointed to the picture she had drawn. She wrote the acronym on the white board. "This is a DNA double helix. DNA stands for *Deoxyribonucleic Acid.*"

Some of the students tried to pronounce it, but it was a tongue-twister for them all. They were content with just jotting down the name in their science composition journals.

Ms. Verdak went on, "DNA makes you who you are. It makes you all unique. That's why some of you are tall and some of you are short."

"So that's why Johnny's the tallest in the class," Lyla said, loudly. She began to understand the concept.

Johnny stood up, waved, and sat back down.

"Or why Megan and I have different eye colors," Samantha added.

"You *all* are correct," Ms. Verdak declared happily. "DNA is also the reason why you look like other members of your family. This is why people might say that you look like your parents or other siblings, meaning your brothers or sisters."

"Do I have a big head?" Lyla asked, raising her hand.

Ms. Verdak thought it was an odd question. "Why do you ask Lyla?"

"Because everyone says my big-headed brother and I look alike," she answered.

A chorus of laughs and giggles rippled through the room.

"Quiet down, everyone," Ms. Verdak ordered them, but only after chuckling too. "I'm sure they're referring to other physical traits. As I was saying, the DNA that you receive from your parents contributes to who you will physically become as a person. Nearly everything about you is based on the structure of your DNA." Ms. Verdak once again directed everyone's attention to the whiteboard. "Within this double helix are instructions for all of the physical characteristics of a person."

She turned to face the class and said, "Now, we're going to do a class activity. I want everyone to choose a partner."

The classroom was suddenly bursting with activity and the racket of moving desks. Samantha rotated hers to join it with Lyla's. Both girls gave each other happy smiles.

Mary raised her hand. "I don't have a partner, Ms. Verdak."

"Johnny is by himself," said Ms. Verdak.

"Do I have to?" Mary protested, displeased with Ms. Verdak's response. "I would rather work by myself."

"Yes, you do," insisted Ms. Verdak as she held up her grade book. "The only way you get a grade is by working with a partner."

Irritated, Mary dragged her desk across the room, leaving a scratched trail on the waxed tile floor.

"OK, class." Ms. Verdak recaptured their attention. "In your groups, I want you all to write down as many physical characteristics as you can think of that are contributed to your DNA." She opened her top desk drawer and took out a white timer. The timer knob clicked as she turned it. "You have fifteen minutes to finish."

The class revved up to write.

"Start now!" Ms. Verdak announced.

The children were busy as bees, crafting their lists.

"DING!" Fifteen quick minutes went by, and the noise gradually stopped.

"I want each group to come up to the front of the class and share what they have done," Ms. Verdak instructed. "You have two minutes to present your lists."

Some students were excited and the rest were filled with nervousness.

"Who's first?" Ms. Verdak asked, her eyes roving around the classroom.

Lyla and Samantha volunteered. They strolled up to the front of the class. Lyla held out their paper for both of them to see, and they took turns naming words from their list.

"Eyes."

"Skin complexion."

"Shoe size."

"Height."

When the girls finished, Ms. Verdak congratulated them. "Great job!" She was impressed by how well they worked together. Lyla and Samantha jumped in the air and gave each other a high five before walking back to their seats.

"Who's next?" asked Ms. Verdak, after recording their grade.

Mary stood up quickly and headed to the front. "Come on!" she ordered Johnny.

Once at the front of the class, Mary called out

so many words, the class couldn't keep up. They didn't even know they had that many body parts.

Johnny stood there as the paper holder and didn't say one word. That was his way of cooperating. They too got praise from Ms. Verdak when they were done.

When the presentations were over, Ms. Verdak assigned the homework. "I want you to go home, pick a family member, and compare and contrast yourselves," she said. "Write down how you and your family member are *similar* and *different*."

"RING!" It was time to switch classrooms and an avalanche of students poured out into the hallway and scattered to their next classes.

It was recess and because the monkey bars were being renovated the Troops had to gather at a new location. They decided to meet by the climbing wall, a new addition to the playground.

Mary came running to join them. "Can I play

with you all?" she asked.

"We're not playing," Nick said. "Can't you see we're in a state of emergency?" he added, hysterically.

Mary was baffled. "State of emergency...about what?"

"Didn't you watch the news last night?" asked Samantha.

"I thought everyone was glued to their tubevisions," Megan added.

Lyla was not taking part in the conversation because she was searching for a word in her pocket dictionary. She found it and said, "We have to be *proactive*."

"What does that mean?" Samantha turned away from the conversation to ask.

"It means that we can't sit on our rumps and not do anything about not getting our new library," explained Lyla. "Especially after all we went through for the Li'berry Fruit!"

"We'll just call ourselves Team Proactive," Samantha said with a smile.

Lyla liked Samantha's humor. "Well, this

team needs to come up with some proactive solutions."

"I have an idea," Nick said.

All eyes were on him, especially Samantha's. She expected Nick to say something crazy.

"Why don't we get the mayor to turn City Hall into a library?" Nick suggested.

"And where would City Hall go?" Megan asked.

"I didn't think that far, yet," Nick admitted.

"Jeez, Nick...it figures," Samantha said.

Lyla came to Nick's defense. "At least Nick is trying to fix the problem." She patted him on the shoulder. "Does anyone have any other ideas?"

Mary chimed in. "So...why couldn't he build the library?" she asked.

"The town is broke!" Nick answered.

"You're telling me that the town doesn't have any money?" she asked, looking around at the other Troops for confirmation.

"Will you tell her I'm telling the truth," said Nick to Megan.

"None!" Megan affirmed, turning towards Mary and shaking her head back and forth.

"Zippo," added Samantha, making a zero with the thumb and first finger of her left hand.

"So now you see why we're having a meeting," Lyla said, looking at Mary. "It's going to be up to us to get our new library!" Lyla sounded like a coach motivating her basketball team, when it was down two points and needing a basket, with only a few seconds left in the game.

Everyone was charged. They didn't have a solution, but they were ready to take on the challenge. Ms. Verdak came onto the playground and announced that it was time to line up.

"Troops!" Lyla yelled to get everyone's attention. "Meet me at my tree house tomorrow at noon."

Mary was waiting for someone to invite her too, but no one said a word. She dredged up the courage to ask, "Me too?"

The Troops looked at Lyla for the go-ahead.

"Sure," Lyla said.

A huge smile brightened Mary's face.

3

Lyla's Idea

Saturday, the Troops rode their bikes to Lyla's house and arrived exactly on time. They were anxious to start looking for ways to raise money to build their library. They parked their bikes on the front sidewalk and waited for Mary on the porch before going in.

"Where is she?" Megan asked, looking down one end of the street.

"Beats me," said Nick, shrugging his shoulders.

Samantha looked the other way and saw her strutting toward the house. "Here she comes."

Mary was happy to be included. She wore her special rainbow-colored headband for the occasion. She had walked past Lyla's house a hundred times, always curious about how the inside of the tree house looked. Today was the day that she would get to find out.

The Troops were just as delighted to see Mary as she was to see them. They greeted her with cheers and hugs. Before one of them could press the bell, the front door flew open. "Hey, Troops... and Mary!" Lyla welcomed them.

"Hey, Lyla," they all responded.

"Come on in." She waved her hand for them to enter.

The Troops stampeded into the kitchen just as Mrs. Lyte removed a tray of fresh-baked cookies from the oven and placed them on the counter. She greeted everyone with a hospitable smile. "Hi, kids."

"Hi, Mrs. Lyte," everyone replied.

"I just *love* that smell," said Nick sticking his nose up in the air and taking a long sniff.

"You kids are just in time to try my new recipe—oatmeal-raisin cookies," Lyla's mom said.

Nick was drooling, his tongue sticking out of

his mouth.

"And what's your name?" Mrs. Lyte asked, turning to Mary.

"My name's Mary, Mary Englemouth."

"She's in my class," Lyla added.

"It's nice to meet you, Mary," Mrs. Lyte said and shook her hand.

"Thank you, ma'am," Mary said with a happy smile.

Just then, Lyla's dad raced down the stairs. "Are those delicious cookies ready yet?" he

asked, oblivious to Lyla and her friends.

"Your daughter has company," Mrs. Lyte pointed out.

"Oh, I'm sorry," Mr. Lyte apologized. "Hi, Troops...*A-tten-tion!*" he called out with a theatrical salute.

It was as if Lyla had been bitten by an embarrassment bug. "Ahhh...Dad!"

Her mom stepped in and asked, "Weren't you watching America's Next Top Mechanic?"

"I sure was," he answered. "And, the commercial should be over." Mr. Lyte scooped up a plateful of cookies and headed back upstairs.

"Thanks, Mom," Lyla said, grateful that she was saved from any further humiliation.

"Everyone can get cookies, and there's milk in the fridge," her mom said. Then she left to go upstairs as well.

"Lyla, your mom is the best baker ever," Mary expressed as she chomped away and savored every bite.

"You can say that again!" Cookie crumbs circled Nick's mouth as he drowned his cookies in milk.

"Slow down, Nick!" Lyla said. "Those cookies aren't going anywhere."

Nick pointed to his belly. "Yes they are. Right down here."

"I can't eat any more," said Megan. She gave her half-eaten cookie to Samantha.

They all watched Nick eat the last morsel of his oatmeal-raisin treat. "Done!" he announced, wiping his mouth with his bare arm.

That was the signal for everyone to head to the tree house. After putting their dirty dishes in the sink, they went out into the backyard with Lyla leading the way. When they reached the tree house, Lyla stopped dead in her tracks. "Wait!" she said, blocking the path.

"What's wrong?" Samantha was bewildered.

"Before we let Mary enter the tree house, she has to go through an initiation," explained a serious Lyla.

"For what?" Nick asked. He was puzzled, much like everyone else.

"To be an official Troop," Lyla answered. "No

outsider has *ever* been allowed to enter our sacred grounds."

The Troops glanced at each other as they finally caught on to what Lyla was talking about. "Oh yeah, you're right!"

"Initiation?" Mary was surprised and unprepared.

"Troops, gather around." Lyla was in command at the head of the pack.

Mary instinctively followed.

Nick looked at her and said, "Not you."

"I forgot," she said, an innocent look plastered on her face.

The Troops huddled away from the tree to discuss the initiation process (or to make one up).

Nick whispered, "Sooo...what's an initiation?"

"It's something Mary has to do to be one of us," Lyla explained.

"Like a test?" Megan guessed, wrinkling her eyebrows.

"Exactly," Lyla said.

"So what should the test or initiation be?" Samantha asked.

I'deyah Ricketts

"Well in a book I read, in order for boys to become men they are sent to live in the wilderness for six months to survive on their own," Lyla explained. "In the book, they called it a coming of age."

"That's cruel," said Megan. "They'll be eaten alive by all types of wild animals."

"Yeah, that's a coming of crazy," Nick agreed.

Samantha popped her head up from the pack and looked around. "Well, there's no wilderness in Coverfield, so we can scratch that idea."

Lyla was upset that they had all blasted what she said. "That wasn't an idea!" she uttered, her voice rising slightly. "It was just an example."

"Sorry!" the Troops apologized together.

Then Lyla thought of an easy task for Mary to undertake. "We'll just have her balance books on top of her head."

"I think that's a lot better," Megan was pleased with Lyla's proposal.

"Simple," smiled Nick. "But, I like it."

Samantha was on board as well. "What if they fall?" she wondered, taking a peek over her

45

shoulder at Mary.

"Then, she will remain a common citizen!" Lyla said.

"OK!" agreed the Troops and turned with smiles on their faces.

"All right, Mary," Lyla began eagerly. "In order to be a Troop, you have to balance books on top of your head."

Mary's eyes wandered from Troop to Troop to see if everyone was on the same page. "How many?" she asked when no one spoke against the task.

All eyes fell on Lyla for guidance. "Ummm!" she thought about it for a few seconds and said, "Four."

"And for *one* minute," added Samantha, holding up one finger.

Mary promptly accepted the challenge. "Nick, go get the books," Lyla said, pointing to the tree house.

He took off, climbed up into the tree house, and collected the first four books he could find.

"Help me out," he shouted from up top. The

Samantha pointed to the corner. "What about those books?"

"Good idea," Lyla said. Both Lyla and Samantha gathered the books and stacked them to act as a seat for Mary. She sat on top of the books, and the meeting started immediately.

"Look, guys," Lyla began, "with all we went through, we're going to find a way for this town to have a new library. We got this town to start reading books and we are *going* to get our library no matter what it takes."

"But the mayor needs money," Megan reminded them, looking doubtful. "How are we going to come up with a million dollars?"

"Yeah...we're only *oneinaires*," Nick said.

Samantha looked dazed. "What's that?"

"It means we're rich with one dollar bills," Nick responded, holding up one finger to emphasize his definition.

Everyone laughed.

"That was funny," Mary commented. "Nick, I didn't know you were a comedian."

"He's not," Samantha added quickly. "He only

says something funny once in a blue moon."

"I'm injured by all of this hating," Nick joked, directing his response to Samantha. "I need hater-aid." He began laughing at his own joke.

Turning Nick's first joke into a suggestion, Lyla said, "Well, I guess we all can save one dollar a week."

Nick immediately stopped laughing. "I'm saving up for an action figure, Superman's arch nemesis Lex Luthor," he explained. "I have five dollars already. If I give a dollar a week, it will take me forever to get Lex."

Samantha calculated numbers in her head. "Guys, I don't think that will be enough. That's only twenty dollars a month together. It will take us over four and a half thousand years to save enough money to get this town to build the library."

"That's way too long," agreed the Troops.

"So where can we get a million dollars?" Lyla asked. She was starting to get discouraged.

"If only money grew on trees like Li'berry Fruit," Mary blurted out.

"Yes!" Lyla replied, grinning.

Mary was flattered, without knowing exactly what she had done that was so terrific. "Thanks for what?"

"D...N...A!" Lyla sounded out the acronym slowly.

"DNA?" the other Troops asked, all at the same time, confused. Four pairs of huge eyes stared at Lyla with wonder.

"How is DNA going to help us?" Megan asked, sounding a little excited. "Please, please, please tell us!" she insisted, shaking Lyla's shoulders back and forth.

"Number one, stop shaking me, and number two, what did Ms. Verdak say about DNA?" she asked.

Samantha remembered. "She said DNA makes us who we are."

Lyla nodded, then added, "Or what something becomes...right?"

Everyone nodded in agreement.

"It just came to me," Lyla continued explaining with wide eyes and a high-pitched voice. "We can grow a money tree from the Li'berry Tree's DNA."

"How?" asked Mary. Her curios-o-meter was off the charts.

"If we extracted the DNA from the Li'berry Tree and combined it with money it might grow a money tree. Then we can take the money off the tree and give it to Mayor Crinkle to pay for the construction of the new library." Lyla waited impatiently for their responses.

"You're insane!" Nick concluded, throwing up his hands.

"That's impossible!" Megan agreed with Nick, as always.

Being the new member, Mary was cautious about sharing her opinion. She didn't want to choose sides.

"This is Coverfield," Lyla stated. "I'm surprised you all would doubt that something strange could happen. Anything is possible where we live."

Samantha was always supportive. "It wouldn't hurt to try. What do we have to lose?"

There was a dead silence in the tree house.

"Nothing!" Samantha added.

"I guess," Nick said, even though he was still wavering on the idea of growing a money tree.

"Yeah, I guess we could give it a try." Once again Megan followed behind Nick.

Lyla cracked a smile.

"So what do we need to do, Lyla?" Mary asked.

"The DNA is contained somewhere in that tree," Lyla said. "First, we have to find out where, and, as a matter of fact, I think I might know where to find the answer. I'll be right back."

Lyla scrambled out of the tree house, ran into her house, and grabbed a thick black book. She returned to the tree house and slammed the book down right in the center of the table, shaking it.

"What a big book!" marveled the Troops.

"It's an encyclopedia," Lyla explained. "This one goes from *R* to *T*." She showed them its spine. Lyla flipped the book open and followed the letter tabs to the letter *T*. She found the word tree and read the information silently as the Troops waited patiently. "Great!" Lyla was smiling from ear to ear.

53

"What is it Lyla?" Samantha asked, eager to hear what she had found out.

Lyla read with her finger guiding her eyes. "'Tree sap is the sticky, gooey fluid produced by a tree. It is full of minerals, nutrients, water, and sugar that makes it a little sweet.'" She looked up. "It says that some people use it to make homemade syrup."

"Yummy," Nick said, licking his lips.

"The DNA has to be found in the tree sap," said Lyla."

"How do we get the sap out of the tree?" Mary asked.

Lyla continued reading. "'The sap is found in the tree trunk and oozes out through a hole in the trunk.'"

Nick began to have doubts about Lyla's idea again. "Well that's not going to work."

"Why?" Lyla asked, disappointed with Nick's skeptical attitude.

He explained. "When Mayor Crinkle tried to chop down the Li'berry Tree, his axe didn't do anything to it at all."

"That's right," Lyla said, thinking back. "But he tried to hurt it. We're working for a *good* cause, so I think the Li'berry Tree will allow us to remove some of the sap."

"How do you know that?" questioned Nick, doubtfully. "Are you and the tree BFFs?" He snickered.

"Trust me on this one!" Lyla said.

4

Tap for Sap

"To get the sap out, I'm going to need some tools. Something straight and sharp and something to bang the other tool into the tree," Lyla said, clenching her fist as if she already had one of the tools in her hand.

"What about your dad?" Samantha asked. "He works on cars and stuff, so he should have something."

Lyla thought for a moment and then said, "OK, let me go ask."

The Troops descended from the tree house one by one and waited patiently by the Li'berry Tree as Lyla went inside the house through the back patio doors.

"Dad!" Lyla called out at the top of her voice.

"I'm in here," he called back. It sounded as if he was far away.

Lyla moved toward the sound of his voice, calling out his name. He responded each time. She finally found herself in the garage. "Where are you?" she asked, looking around the garage. She didn't see him at all.

"I'm down here." Mr. Lyte was on a creeper rolled underneath the family van. Lyla only saw his legs, white socks, and shoes sticking out.

"What are you doing?" she asked, squatting down to look at him.

"I'm changing the oil. The van is badly in need of an oil change." He rolled himself further underneath the van. "I should have changed it at the shop a long time ago, but you know how busy I get."

"I know. You should just move your bed there," joked Lyla.

Mr. Lyte's chuckling was drowned out by the sounds of banging and the screwing on and off of bolts. Lyla had to project her voice. "It sure is noisy in here!"

"Noise to you, *but* music to me," he shouted. "So, what do you need?"

"I need a couple of tools," she told him. It felt like they were in a yelling match.

"You need what?" Mr. Lyte paused in his work to hear her clearly.

Lyla lowered the volume of her voice. "A tool that's straight and sharp and one to pound it into something," Lyla explained.

"Look in my toolbox."

Lyla straightened up, and looked around the garage. "Where is it?"

"It's on my work bench." He went back to work, clamping his wrench around a bolt.

Lyla spotted the apple-red toolbox. She went to it, quickly opened it, and went scavenging for the right tools. "These should work!" exclaimed Lyla, giddily, finding a small silver chisel and a hammer with a black rubber handle. "I found what I needed, thanks, Dad!"

"I'm glad I could help," her dad replied. "Can you hand me one of those buckets on the floor to put the oil in?" he asked.

Lyla noticed two blue buckets that were about three feet away from her, one large and the other medium sized. *Buckets! We're definitely going to need something to put the sap in,* she thought. "Dad, can I use one of these buckets?" she asked.

"Of course," answered her dad. "Make sure you bring everything back when you're done."

"I will." Lyla tossed both tools inside a bucket, gave her dad the bigger one, and rushed back to rejoin the rest of the Troops.

"She got them!" cried Mary, the first one to notice Lyla speeding back. "That's great!"

"Perfect! We're ready to go," Nick said. He held out his hands expecting Lyla to hand them over. "Tools...please," he said.

Lyla disregarded Nick's request. "I'm the only one that's going to do the tapping." She dropped the bucket in the grass. The tools jingled inside as it landed.

Nick withdrew his hand and snatched the bucket from off the ground. "Why?" he asked, frowning.

"Because they're my tools and not yours," Lyla answered, as she snatched the bucket back from Nick. She was irritated by his sudden take-charge attitude.

"No," Nick promptly refuted. "They belong to *your* dad."

Samantha knew where this tussle was headed. "Do you two ever get tired of fussing?" she asked, stepping between them.

"No!" both Lyla and Nick answered in unison.

"We'll, I'm tired of it, and I know the rest of us are too!" Samantha said, glaring at her friends.

Mary gave Megan a slight bump to get her attention. "Do they fight like this all the time?" she whispered.

"Yup," Megan whispered back. "And this is a mild day."

Samantha continued refereeing. "We have one goal. And that goal is to get the sap. There're two tools." She took the bucket from Lyla and reached for the chisel, giving it to her to hold. "You use this!" Then she reached for the hammer, grabbed it, and handed it over to Nick. "You pound it with this!" she ordered.

After being forced to establish a working relationship, Lyla led the way to the Li'berry Tree, Nick behind her. "Hi, tree," Lyla said tenderly, rubbing the bark. "We *need* your help. We can't build our new library because we need lots of money."

"A million dollars!" Nick bellowed, interruptting Lyla.

She glared at Nick and said, "Please, I'll do the talking and you do the hammering." Lyla turned back to the tree. "We found a solution, but we need some of your sap, and I hope it's OK with you."

"Excuse me," said Nick. "Are you and the tree finished bonding?" Now he was teasing.

"Yes, we are," responded Lyla. "Are you guys ready to tap for sap?"

"Hey, that rhymes!" Megan pointed out.

"Yeah, that's the poet inside of me," Lyla said, bobbing her head.

"The who?" Mary asked.

"Let's just focus on getting the sap out of the

tree," Lyla said, not wanting to explain herself. "Nick, are you ready to hammer?"

Nick raised the hammer and said, "Yup!"

Lyla raised the chisel and gently placed the edge of the blade against the tree. "Don't hit my hand!" she said to Nick with a warning look.

"Don't worry, I won't," Nick assured her.

Lyla dropped her eyelids out of sheer nervousness. Nick swung his arm back, clutching the hammer tightly, and drove the chisel straight through the tree bark. He banged it five times until the chisel was securely in the tree. "You can open your eyes, now," Nick said, grinning.

Lyla lifted her eyelids and saw the chisel thrust into the Li'berry Tree. She breathed a sigh of relief, then tried twisting the chisel a little, clockwise, clasping it with both hands, but it didn't budge. "I think that should do it," she said to the Troops. Using the tree as leverage, she perched her foot against the tree, and tried pulling the chisel out, but that was no go as well. "Help!" she cried.

The Troops rushed to Lyla's aid. Samantha

pulled on Lyla, Megan pulled on Samantha, Mary pulled on Megan, and Nick pulled on Mary.

"On three," Lyla shouted. "One...two...three...pull! They all tugged together, the chisel came flying out, and the Troops tumbled to the grass like dominos.

When they all got up and looked, they saw they had managed to bore a nice-sized hole. They waited and waited for the sap to flow, but nothing came out.

"Awww, it didn't work!" expressed Mary, disappointed.

"I knew your plan wouldn't work!" Nick exclaimed, feeling let down as well.

"Maybe we did something wrong. So let's find out what it was, and do it better next time," Samantha said, trying to stay optimistic. "Lyla, read the encyclopedia again and see what it says."

Lyla examined the hole and said confidently, "I made sure I read everything."

All of a sudden, a drip of sap hung from the edge of the hole. Unable to hold on for long, it fell to the grass.

"Get the bucket!" Lyla commanded. "See, I told you guys it would work!"

The Troops were ecstatic.

Nick ran and snatched up the bucket and placed it underneath the hole. The sap dripped slowly into the bucket. When it was full, the sap instantly stopped flowing. It was as if the Li'berry Tree was cooperating with the Troops. They gathered around the bucket of sap in amazement.

Nick bent down and dunked his finger in the bucket. He pulled it out with sticky sap all over it.

"What are you doing?" Samantha asked, looking at Nick strangely.

"I'm seeing how it tastes," Nick replied, as if it were a normal thing to do. Then he put his gooey finger in his mouth. "Mmmm!" he murmured. But, when he tried to pull out his finger, it was a struggle. When he finally succeeded, his lips stuck together like they were glued. He muttered something, but the Troops couldn't understand what he was saying.

"I *love* that sap!" Samantha exclaimed, her eyes bright with laughter.

"Why?" Mary asked.

"It got Nick to shut up," Samantha said, clasping her lips shut with her hand.

The girls all laughed.

"So, what do we do now?" Megan asked.

All eyes turned to Lyla for guidance. "Like I said," Lyla began to explain again, "we have to bury the sap with money. Before the tree grew Li'berry Fruit, we found a seed that was stuck in the ground." She looked downward as she remembered. "And maybe that will grow a money seed underground. Then, we can dig up the seed and bury it. And that can grow a huge money tree."

"So, all we need now...is money." Samantha smiled, rubbing her thumb and two fingers together.

"That, I don't have," Lyla said, turning her pockets inside out. All that was there was lint.

The other girls shrugged their shoulders and shook their heads. Then all of their eyes turned to Nick.

"Wooo, finally, my lips are unstuck," Nick bellowed, triumphantly. "Why are you all staring at me?" he asked.

"We *need* your five dollars," Lyla demanded, holding out her hand.

Nick was stunned by the request. "For what?"

Megan explained. "We're going to bury it with the sap to grow the money tree."

"And what am I going to use to buy my action figure?" he asked.

Lyla retrieved her pocket dictionary from the right pocket of her blue jean capris. She flipped the pages and found the word she was searching for in a matter of seconds. She lifted her head and jumped back into the conversation. "Nick, if it works, you'll get *interest* on top of your five dollars."

"I'll get what?" He had absolutely no clue of the meaning of the word.

"If the tree grows money, you'll get more money back." Lyla explained. "That's interest. You can buy Lex, daddy Lex, mommy Lex, and baby Lex. Even grandpa and grandma Lex!"

"I only want Lex Luthor!" Nick said. "And Superman's arch enemy doesn't come with a whole family. He's a bad guy and bad guys are not family men." Nick turned his back on the girls and folded his arms. Lyla's strategy obviously didn't work.

Mary begged with big, blue eyes, "Come on, Nick."

"Yeah, Nick," added Megan. "What are best friends for?"

Samantha joined in. "Yeah, I make fun of you a lot, but you're the only friend I have that's a boy."

The girls couldn't see it, but Nick was starting to blush.

Lyla stood there in silence. The girls were urging Lyla to say something nice about Nick, but she was stubborn. She shook her head as they all stared at her.

Samantha clasped her hands as if she was praying and mouthed, "Pleeease!"

"OK, then!" Lyla unbent. "The Troops wouldn't be complete without you!" she spat out.

He turned around and gave the girls a gigantic grin. "I know you all couldn't live without me!"

They all giggled.

"I'll be right back. Nick hopped on his bike, and rode off home to get the money.

5

Back to the Dumpsite

It seemed like it took Nick forever to return. He peddled up to the house with a nonchalant attitude.

"Nick, you're slower than a snail sleep-crawling," Samantha teased, shaking her head at him.

"I had to do something for my mom," he replied.

Lyla looked at Nick and saw ketchup smeared around his mouth. "Do what? Help her eat turkey burgers?"

"What are you talking about?" he asked in a suspiciously high-pitched voice, while avoiding eye contact with Lyla.

Lyla approached Nick, who was still on his

bike, wiped a little bit of the ketchup off from around his mouth with her finger and showed it to him.

"Oh, you mean that." He smirked.

"For someone so skinny, you sure eat a lot," Samantha said.

"I can't help if I'm a growing boy," Nick retorted, finally dismounting his bike.

"Now that Nick is back, *let's* get to work," said Lyla, wiping the ketchup off on her capri pants. "Hand over the money," she said to Nick, holding her right hand out.

Nick began searching his pockets. "Candy wrapper, nope. Peanuts." He tasted one. "Stale!" He continued rummaging through all the clutter in his pockets. "Tissue. Wait, this isn't it. "Oh, here it is!" He pulled out a crumpled five-dollar bill and handed it over to Lyla.

"Thanks!" she said, and straightened it out on the knee of her capris.

Nick was sad to part with all his savings. Just like the town of Coverfield, he too was now broke.

Mary noticed his sullen demeanor and patted

him on the back. "Everything's going to be OK."

"I'll go get a shovel," said Lyla. She ran off toward the house. When she went into the garage, she saw her dad was underneath the hood of the van. She tapped him on his back, catching him off guard. Startled, he banged his head on the inside of the hood.

"*Ouch!*" he screeched. "Lylaaa!"

"Sorry, Dad."

"It's, OK. What do you need now?" her dad asked, holding the oil dipstick in his hand and

checking the oil level. "Did those tools help you guys with whatever you were doing?

"Yeah, but now I need a shovel," Lyla said, still standing behind him.

Wiping the dipstick clean with an old rag, he asked, "What do you need a shovel for?"

"We're planting seeds," replied Lyla, stretching the truth.

"Last time you planted a seed it *grew* books," her dad said. "What are you trying to grow now...money?"

Lyla was shocked by her dad's question. She didn't know how to respond.

"Now, *that* would be funny!" Mr. Lyte laughed, cracking himself up.

"Yeah, that would be silly," Lyla pretended to be tickled as she gave a fake laugh. *Thank goodness he was only kidding*, she thought.

"The shovel is over there, by the rake." Her dad pointed and ducked his head back under the hood of the van.

Lyla went to the corner of the garage and grabbed the shovel. "Dad, you're the best!" she said, trying to butter him up.

"Yeah, when you need something," he said, pouring a quart of oil inside the engine.

Lyla rushed back to the Troops carrying the shovel. "Let's dig here," she said, finding a spot a few feet away from the tree.

"OK," the Troops agreed.

"Since we only have one shovel, I'll dig first and someone can dig after me," Lyla said. She stuck the shovel into the soft turf, scooped up some dirt, and flung it to the side. She shoveled for ten minutes and stopped. "Who wants to shovel next?"

"I'm not dressed for manual labor," Mary declared. She was wearing a white shirt, a yellow skirt, white socks, and gold flats. "I'll shovel." Samantha volunteered eagerly. She grasped the shovel and started where Lyla had left off. After another ten minutes, she announced that she was done.

Lyla stared down into the hole and determined it was deep enough. "Someone bring the bucket of sap."

Nick went to get to the bucket and hauled it close to the hole.

"Pour the sap into the hole," Lyla instructed him.

Nick did as she directed. Next, Lyla stooped on her knees and cautiously tossed the five dollars in the hole with the sap. She stood back up and said, "Nick you have the honor of plugging up the hole.

"Awesome!" Nick exclaimed proudly. He picked up the shovel and filled the hole with dirt.

"Great job, Nick," said Lyla. Then she went to get the water hose. She drenched the spot until the dirt was moist. "That should do it," she said.

"How are we going to find this spot tomorrow?" Megan asked.

"We need something to stick in the dirt," Samantha suggested. "That way we can find it again."

The Troops spread out around the backyard, searching. Lyla soon found a thin broken branch. "We can use this." She stuck it right on top of the hill of dirt, like a flag announcing their colony.

"Troops, now our job is finally done," she declared.

"How long do we have to wait for the money tree to grow?" Mary asked.

"We'll, the Li'berry Tree grew *overnight*, so...tomorrow," Lyla guessed.

"That sure is fast," Mary said, shocked, thinking it would have taken weeks.

"So, let's report to my house tomorrow, same time," Lyla said, looking at her watch.

Mary was extremely excited. "I don't know about you, guys, but I won't be able to sleep tonight."

The next day the Troops were anxious to see if a seed had grown underground. They all brought their shovels, except for Mary of course. Easily locating the hump of dirt with the stick protruding from the top, they took turns digging. When the hole was exposed, they found the five-dollar bill swimming in the sap.

"Nothing happened!" Megan exclaimed.

"It should have worked!" said Lyla, staring flabbergasted down into the gaping hole.

The Troops could see that Lyla was very disappointed.

Samantha thought back to when they found the Li'berry Fruit seed. "Maybe we need to *go* back to the dumpsite," she suggested "and bury the sap and money there."

"Wait, wait!" Nick yelped. "I don't think that's a good idea. Anyway there's no guarantee that it would work. Maybe it just takes longer to grow a seed than a tree."

Samantha thought about this for a second and said, "Isn't that backward? Before the tree comes the seed."

The thought of going back to the dumpsite pepped up Lyla's mood. She smiled and said, "Let's try it!"

"Come on, guys, that place *stinks*," Nick whined, trying to discourage them.

"Nick, please don't fight us on this one," Lyla said. "This is all part of the mission."

"OK." He yielded to Lyla's request without a

heated battle.

After the Troops had tapped the Li'berry Tree for more sap, Lyla sprinted into the house to get a sandwich bag to hold the sap-saturated five-dollar bill. She told her parents that they were going bike riding. Without questioning, they thought it was the Troops' usual bike outing. Lyla got her bike and attached the red wagon to it. She grabbed the other bucket out of the garage, filled it with water, and put it in the wagon with the bucket of sap and the shovels.

"Don't forget this," Megan said, tossing the stick in the wagon.

The Troops mounted their bikes, except for Mary. Her bike was retired at home on a flat tire. "You can sit on my handle bars," offered Nick.

She thanked him, perched comfortably on the handlebars, and they rode west toward the dumpsite.

High piles of garbage welcomed them long before they arrived at the entrance to the dumpsite, along with barrels from the *Anything Can Grow Laboratory* that were spilling green goop all over the ground.

"Stop!" Mary shrieked. Nick came to a sudden stop, and she jumped off of the handlebars. "I'm not going in there!" she said.

"Why?" Lyla asked, as if there was nothing wrong with visiting a dumpsite.

"Are you kidding me?" Mary said. "Look at this place…it's a dump!"

"Well, it *is* a dumpsite," Samantha said, sarcastically.

Nick was relishing the moment. He had a smirk on his face. "I told you this place is stinkgusted!" he said.

"Mary, please don't be like Nick," Lyla said.

"Well, call me Mary Nelson," she replied, sarcastically. "And I'm not setting a foot in there."

Megan gave a slight grunt. She didn't like that name since she was fond of Nick.

"Because we're the only ones with sense," continued Mary. "I'm going home!" She turned around, ready to walk all the way.

Lyla hopped off her bike and jumped in front of Mary and said, "Are you a Troop or not?" She pointed at her. "Because us Troops look in the face of danger and laugh loudly. For years, they called girls too prissy. If you go home, you're not turning your back only on us, but you're turning your back on *all* women who sacrificed for us girls to have an equal opportunity to show how tough we are. Go in there for the sake of girlhood!"

Megan turned to Samantha and whispered, "Where does she get this stuff from?"

"Books, I guess," answered Samantha.

Inspired by the Lyla's speech, Mary smiled, turned back, and faced the dumpsite entrance bravely. "Well, I'm a Troop," she declared, "so let's go!"

Nick frowned. "Shoot!" He was deprived of his last means of escape.

They cautiously walked their bikes into the dumpsite, staying clear of the goop on the ground.

"Let's try over there," Lyla pointed beyond the largest pile of garbage.

Megan got their attention by yelling, "Hey, look over there."

"Where?" The Troops asked looking in

different directions.

She pointed to a large heap of tubevisions. "Over there."

After removing the tubevisions from the classrooms, Mayor Crinkle had transported them to the dumpsite hoping *they* would slowly decay.

"So that's where they discarded them," Lyla said with a smile.

"Good riddance to them all," Samantha said.

"There's the one that was in our classroom." Nick pointed one out. It was lying at the bottom of the pile, battered, with a broken screen.

"Memories," both Lyla and Mary said, looking at each other.

Lyla reflected. "Just think... we were enemies."

"And now, we're friends," Mary said. "And I'm a Troop."

"Well, we're all friends," added Megan.

The Troops all took a minute to ponder their bond and their friendship.

"Well, Troops, let's continue searching for a spot," Lyla commanded, ending the trip down memory lane. They walked around the large pile of garbage until they came to a spot that was suitable for digging. They parked their bikes and removed the shovels and buckets from the wagon.

Since they had more shovels, it took them a lot less time to replant the five dollars and the sap. Lyla poured the water on the mound and marked it with the same stick.

"How are we going to check on the seed tomorrow?" Mary asked. "Tomorrow is Monday," she added, "we have school."

They had all forgotten that the next day was a school day.

"Oh, yeah...you're right," Megan said.

"I can't wait for next weekend!" Mary said, suddenly anxious to come back the dumpsite.

The wheels in Lyla's head started to turn. She was thinking of a plan and began biting her fingernails. She spat out a piece of nail and said, "After school, everyone tell your parents you're coming over my house to work on a science project. And we'll meet up at Program Park."

"And what are you going to tell your mom and dad?" Samantha wondered.

"I'll think of something," Lyla uttered confidently.

"I guess that could work," said Nick.

"Yeah, that would work for me." Megan agreed.

"It's not the best plan, but it's a plan," Samantha said.

"Sure!" Mary agreed too.

"Well, then, it's settled. Tomorrow, we'll meet

up at Program Park," Lyla said. They hopped on their bikes and headed out of the dumpsite.

6
ELUA

Monday, at 6:30 in the morning, Mr. Butler stopped the black stretch limo in front of a closed City Hall. He got out, walked around to the back passenger door, and opened it for Mayor Crinkle. "Do you need me for anything else, sir?" he asked.

"I'll call you if I need you," Mayor Crinkle replied as he got out of the car, carrying his brown leather briefcase.

"I'll be in the garage washing the limo," Mr. Butler said as he shut the car door. He hopped back in and drove around to the back.

Before he could climb the stairs to the front double doors, Mayor Crinkle was startled by a sudden tap on his lower back. He spun around and found a strange man, shorter than himself, standing before him. *Wow, someone shorter than me!* Mayor Crinkle thought, looking down.

"Good morning, Mayor," the man greeted. He was wearing an elephant-gray suit and was lugging a black briefcase with the letters ELUA printed on it. He extended his arm, giving Mayor Crinkle a firm handshake.

"How can I help you?" asked Mayor Crinkle, wondering just who the pint-size stranger was.

The man handed Mayor Crinkle a fancy business card and introduced himself. "My name is Stan Johnson. I'm the president of the Environmental Land Use Association."

Mayor Crinkle glanced at the card, impressed by the organization's long name. "The ELUA, how about we meet in my office," he said and led the way into the building. He retrieved two keys on a skinny silver chain attached to one of his belt loops. "Come on in," he said, opening the front door. The lobby was decorated with plush sofas, a few armchairs, and a charcoal gray rug on the tiled floor. They strolled past two elevators down a long hallway before reaching Mayor Crinkle's office suite.

"My new secretary should be here shortly," Mayor Crinkle said. He used the second key to open his office door."

"Nice!" said Mr. Johnson. He was highly impressed by the look of the mayor's office.

"Please, take a seat." Mayor Crinkle gestured to one of the black chairs in front of his desk. He placed his briefcase on the floor next to a box with campaign materials and sat behind his desk with a slight slouch. "And what is it you would like to talk to me about?"

"I saw your news broadcast," Mr. Johnson began, his feet dangling above the floor. "And the ELUA is *not* happy with the pile of books sitting on the vacant land."

Mayor Crinkle straightened up. "They're books!" he sputtered, realizing this was not a feel-good meeting.

"Books that are an eyesore," snapped Mr. Johnson.

"I'm sorry you don't like to read," Mayor Crinkle said. "But we don't have anywhere to put them."

Mr. Johnson was insulted. "I will have you know that I'm a very proficient reader. Matter of fact, I'm on chapter five of *A Wrinkle in Time*, but my reading habits are not the topic of this discussion."

"Mr. Johnson," Mayor Crinkle said. "You saw my news item two nights ago, right?"

"Yes," Mr. Johnson answered, not sure where

Mayor Crinkle was going with the question.

"So as you know, I'm trying to build a library, and I have nowhere else to store those books while we try to raise the money."

Mr. Johnson leaned forward in the chair, and raised his voice. "I truly understand your dilemma, but with the rain and the snow that will be coming in winter it's just not good to have those books stacked sky-high on that land."

"Oh, I get it now," said Mayor Crinkle. Then he began to smile. "Thank you!"

His sudden calm baffled Mr. Johnson. "Thank me for what?" he asked.

"For the million dollar check you're going to write to help the city build a new library." The grin on the mayor's face widened.

"I don't like your offensive attitude," Mr. Johnson said. He stood up. "I see that it's an election year." He glanced at some of the campaign materials. "If you don't clear that land of those books, I will do *all* I can to make sure you're not reelected as mayor of Coverfield."

Mayor Crinkle stood and said, "Does this

conclude our meeting?"

Mr. Johnson walked toward the door, turned around, and replied, "Yes, and thank you for your time."

"Wasted time!" Mayor Crinkle grumbled.

"Have a good day." Mr. Johnson went out of the door.

"For you, it probably is," Mayor Crinkle muttered. Without showing it, he was just as worried as Lyla and the Troops. *What am I going to do?* he thought. *This is not how I wanted to start my morning.*

"Mr. Butler," Mayor Crinkle called on the office phone.

"Yes, sir," Mr. Butler answered, holding a sponge soaked with suds.

Mayor Crinkle told him to bring the limo around. In no time the limo arrived dripping wet, and the mayor jumped in. "Take me to the Lyte's house," he instructed, before he could even shut the limo door.

"That guy must have ruffled your feathers, sir," Mr. Butler said, with some concern.

"He sure did," Mayor Crinkle said in answer.

The limo sped off and twenty minutes later they were parked in front of the Lyte's house.

Mayor Crinkle rang the bell.

"Who is it?" Lyla asked, waiting by the door for her dad to take her to school.

"It's Mayor Crinkle. I would like to speak with your father," the mayor said.

Surprised by the mayor's unannounced visit that *early* in the morning, Lyla opened the door and politely let him in. She turned around and bellowed at the top of her voice, "Dad, Mayor Crinkle wants to talk to you!" She then turned back to the mayor. "Hi, Mayor Crinkle," she said.

"Hello there, Lyla," he replied. "I'm sorry about the library. I'm disappointed too. It's just that..."

"The town doesn't have enough money," Lyla interrupted, finishing Mayor Crinkle's sentence.

Mayor Crinkle nodded his head sadly. "I'm

trying everything I can to raise the money," he said. "I have faith that it will happen."

As if that was his cue, Mr. Lyte rushed down the stairs wearing his work uniform and feeling awkward about the mayor's unexpected visit. But he welcomed Mayor Crinkle with a handshake. "Hello there, Mayor Crinkle."

"Hello," said the mayor. "So, how's the auto repair shop going? We still miss you as our camera guy."

"It's going great!" smiled Mr. Lyte. "Everything is running very smoothly and efficiently."

"That's wonderful!" Mayor Crinkle replied with a hint of delight in his voice.

Lyla was still standing near the adults. Mayor Crinkle didn't want Lyla to hear what he had to say to Mr. Lyte, so he asked, "Is there somewhere we can talk in private?"

"Well, sadly I don't have an office," Mr. Lyte said.

"Anywhere is fine," Mayor Crinkle replied.

"We can..." Mr. Lyte's eyes scanned the room

for a place private enough to talk, "… go into the garage, but it has to be quick so I can get Lyla to school on time."

"That's perfect," Mayor Crinkle answered, pleased. "And I won't take up too much of your time."

"Lyla, I'll be right back," her dad said, taking Mayor Crinkle into the garage, closing the door behind them. "I'm sorry there's nowhere to sit," he said.

Mayor Crinkle leaned against the family van. "No problem. Like I told you, I won't be long."

Mr. Lyte asked nervously, "Is there something wrong, sir? All of those years I worked for you, this is the first time you've been inside of my home."

Mayor Crinkle began to explain the reason for his visit. "What I have to tell you is extremely important!" He took his handkerchief out of his suit pocket, removed his eyeglasses, wiped the lenses, and put them back on.

Their conversation was loud enough that it was broadcast into the hallway where Lyla was standing by the garage door, eavesdropping.

Mayor Crinkle went on, "This morning the president of the ELUA came to my office."

"What's that?" asked Mr. Lyte puzzled.

"I apologize. It stands for the Environmental Land Use Association," explained Mayor Crinkle. "He informed me that they are not happy with the mountain of books piled up on the vacant land. And I must say that he was a rude and obnoxious little fellow."

Mr. Lyte was thrown aback by the news. "But do they know your intentions to build a new library and that the town does not have the money?" Mr. Lyte wasn't sure if the mayor forgot to mention that.

Mayor Crinkle nodded his head, "Yes, I did tell him."

"What did the man say?" Mr. Lyte asked.

"It didn't make a difference," Mayor Crinkle exclaimed. "He wants those books *gone.*"

"So, what should I do?" Mr. Lyte asked, worriedly rubbing the back of his neck.

Mayor Crinkle took a deep breath and said,

"At this moment, I don't know. If I don't come up with a solution for those books, I could lose my job!"

Both Mr. Lyte and Lyla were stunned.

She heard every word on the other side of the garage door. *Oh no*! thought Lyla. *That's not fair!*

"I'm sorry that I put you in this situation," Mr. Lyte said. "I feel responsible since my daughter planted the seed in our backyard that grew the Li'berry Tree. If I could stop the Li'berry Tree from growing books every day I would."

"We're in this together," Mayor Crinkle declared, putting his hand on Mr. Lyte's shoulder.

"There has to be another way to please the ELUA," Mr. Lyte said.

"All they want is for those books to vanish." Mayor Crinkle reiterated. "I guess not *everyone* sees the value of building a library for the town."

"We will do all we can to help you raise the money, I promise," said Mr. Lyte.

"Thank you," The mayor still looked troubled. "Well, I'll be going now."

Mr. Lyte pressed the garage door opener mounted on the wall by the light switch and said, "You don't have to go out that way, sir. You can leave through there." He pointed toward the big garage door as it rose up. "Just watch your step."

"Tell your wife hello," said Mayor Crinkle as he left.

"If it's not one thing it's another," Mr. Lyte said to himself, watching the limo drive away.

7

The Secret Name

After meeting up at Program Park, the Troops headed straight to the dumpsite on their bikes, with their cinch sacks strapped to their backs. This time Mary rode along with the caravan instead of hitching a ride on Nick's handlebars. She had asked her dad to fix her bike as soon as she got home from the dumpsite the day before. It was hot pink with a matching seat, decorated with pink and white streamers on the handlebars, and had a brown wicker basket that she carried her books in.

"What did you tell your mom," Samantha asked as she rode alongside Lyla. She was curious to hear what Lyla told her.

Lyla turned her head at a slight angle to face Samantha. "I told her that I was going bike riding with you," she said.

"So you told her *we* were going to the dumpsite to dig up a seed that's supposed to grow money?" she asked.

"Nope," replied Lyla, turning her eyes back to the road. "I hate that I didn't tell my mom everything, but we have to see if it worked."

Samantha thought about it for a second and said, "Well, I guess you are riding with me."

The Troops arrived at the dumpsite and wasted no time going in. They dismounted their bikes and walked them to the spot where they had buried the sap and money. It seemed like there was even more green goop covering the ground.

"This is worse than it was yesterday," Mary exclaimed, looking disgusted.

"You're right!" Nick said. "Why did I let you guys talk me into this?"

"It should be just around that pile of garbage," Lyla said, pointing at huge trash bags bulging at

the seams.

As soon as they made it around the corner, they stopped in surprise.

"Wow!" everyone cried. They all were in awe. They couldn't believe what they were seeing. A

towering tree with money dangling from its many branches had grown *overnight*. They ran toward the tree and circled it, stunned, trampling over money as they went.

Lyla looked closely. "Look," she said with

excitement. "They're all five dollar bills!"

"We're rich!" Nick shouted at the top of his voice. "I can buy the whole Justice League and their arch enemies!"

"This is better than I could have ever imagined!" Lyla cried. She scooped up piles of money and flung them in the air, becoming even giddier when they rained down on her. "Thank you, thank you, thank you!" she sang. "We are finally going to get our library. I thought we would find a seed, but we found a money tree. All the tree has to do is keep growing money. There will be a million dollars in no time."

Samantha threw herself to the ground and started rolling around in the money.

Mary was frozen with shock. Her eyes were wide open and she was gawking at the money tree. She thought, *This is unreal, this is unreal!*

Megan was jumping in the air and plucking money off of the branches. "Five dollars...ten dollars...fifteen dollars...twenty dollars...twenty five dollars!" she counted out loud.

The Troops were ecstatic. Nothing could have

prepared them for this moment.

"Lyla, you're a genius!" cried Samantha. She got up with five dollar bills stuck to her clothes and gave Lyla a ginormous hug.

"I just *love* when a plan works!" Lyla gloated a bit. "We've got to show this to Mayor Crinkle! We can most definitely build the library!" Finalizing the plan was all Lyla could think about.

"Let's go shopping first," Nick said. "We can buy anything we want. We're now *fiveionares!*"

"I could buy that cute yellow dress and that matching headband and that purple, striped top, along with those black, patent-leather shoes," Mary said, pacing back and forth and using her fingers to tally the number of clothing items she wanted.

Megan stood there in a dream state, smiling. Then she began yelling out loud, "I can. I can. I could build the first dance studio in Coverfield! I could teach ballet, hip-hop, tap, even square dancing."

"Guys, guys!" shouted Lyla, trying to get their attention. But they all were sidetracked by the money.

"I *love* you money tree," Samantha exclaimed, hugging it. "I'm buying everyone in my family something, even Pinky." (Pinky was their pet poodle.)

"Stop!" Lyla screamed, nearly popping their eardrums. "I said, Stop!"

Everyone stopped and looked at Lyla with dazed eyes.

"Look at you all!" she said, pointing to each one of them. "You're all going crazy! The money is not for us. It's to give to Mayor Crinkle to build the library."

"Wait a minute," Nick said with a hand full of money. "You promised that I would get interest on my money. He shoved the money into Lyla's face. "So this is it."

"I'm sorry I told you that," Lyla said. "At the time, I would have told you anything to get you to give up your five dollars for the mission."

"So you basically lied to me," Nick argued, giving her an accusing look.

"I like to think of it as persuading you," Lyla

replied.

Nick looked displeased. "You'll never change," he said, shaking his head back and forth. "But I'm taking back the money I gave." He quickly deposited five dollars in his pocket.

"No problem," said Lyla and she went on with getting them all focused. "We have a task to complete. And it doesn't involve going shopping."

Mary had a tiny smirk on her face, holding some of the five-dollar bills behind her back. "I have a birthday coming up. It wouldn't hurt if we did a little shopping."

"No!" Lyla said, sternly. "If Mayor Crinkle doesn't get the money to build the library, he's going to lose his job."

"How?" Megan asked.

Lyla explained. "Mayor Crinkle visited my dad this morning to tell him that a man from an organization wants the books removed from the vacant land or else he's going to make sure he's not the mayor anymore."

The news troubled the Troops. "That's awful!" Mary said.

"The money that grew on the tree is not for us to go on a spending tree...I mean spree," Lyla quickly corrected herself.

Samantha was feeling a little embarrassed. She stepped forward. "Lyla's right. Look at us." she said, looking around. "We're out of control. We forgot all about what we said we were going to use the money for."

Megan was overcome with humiliation as well. She slowly walked up to Lyla with her head down. Five dollars bills fell from her hand with every step she took. "I'm still on board," she said as she picked up her head and looked Lyla in the eyes.

Lyla smiled.

"OK, OK," Mary said, surrendering and dropping her money. "My birthday gift can wait."

Next, they all turned to Nick, waiting for his response.

"Can we at least buy something to eat?" he asked timidly.

"Sure," agreed Lyla. "That's reasonable. Now let's gather some money to show Mayor Crinkle."

They scattered, grabbed their cinch sacks, and began loading them with money. All of a sudden, Lyla stopped and searched through her pocket dictionary.

"What word are you looking for now?" Megan asked, pushing money down into her sack.

Lyla began to explain as she searched, "If money made *us* act like we lost our minds we should probably come up with a secret name to hide the money tree from others."

"Like Li'berry Fruit," Nick said, picking up five dollars bills from the ground.

"Yeah," Lyla agreed, nodding her head.

"What word did you find?" Samantha inquired. Curious, she walked over to Lyla and peeked over her shoulder into the dictionary.

"I haven't found one yet," Lyla replied, flipping the pages.

The other Troops were so interested in coming up with a secret name that they stopped filling their sacks.

"Cool!" Lyla exclaimed, her eyes growing bigger. She had found a word and shared it with

the Troops, "What do you guys think about this word?"

"Our ears are open," Samantha said.

"*Loot*," said Lyla, still looking at the dictionary, silently reading the definition over and over.

The Troops repeated the strange sounding word, "Loot!"

"It's a synonym for money," Lyla explained as she looked up at them. "We can call the money tree...a...Loot Tree."

"If I didn't know what loot meant then no one else will, so let's use it," said Nick.

"It's cool with me," Samantha agreed.

Megan and Mary looked at each other and nodded. "We like it," they said in unison.

"Then it's a done deal," Lyla confirmed, closing her pocket dictionary. "From now on we'll refer to the money tree as a Loot Tree."

"Great." The Troops were pleased with the new name.

"So, let's keep stuffing," Lyla said as she picked up her cinch sack. They all resumed packing their sacks until they were full of five-dollar bills.

"That's it for me!" Nick said, throwing his sack over his back.

"Me too."

"And me."

"Yup, I can't fit any more either," Lyla said closing her sack too. "Let's get out of here!"

They all hopped on their bikes, letting up the kickstands, and rode away happily, out of the dumpsite.

8

The Waitress

A few blocks from Knob Hill and City Hall, Nick suddenly hit his brakes and came to a screeching stop. His eyes locked on Coverfield's best restaurant, Dish Dining. "I say we eat there," he suggested, rubbing his tummy.

The others stopped pedaling, taking a curved path to land beside Nick.

"Fine with me," Samantha said.

"I *love* their burgers!" Megan exclaimed, already drooling.

The rest gladly agreed.

They parked their bikes in front and walked inside the restaurant where an aroma was swirling through the air. Each took a whiff of the delicious, mouth-watering scent, looking like they were hypnotized. They seated themselves at a vacant booth and placed their cinch sacks underneath the table. They began calling out the food they wanted to eat.

"I want pizza!" Nick said, without even looking at the menu sitting on the red-and-white checkered tablecloth.

"I want a cheeseburger!" said Megan. "With extra pickles."

Lyla suggested getting cheese fries. She was the first to pick up her menu and glance at the side order section.

Samantha shook her head. "I'd rather just have plain fries. Cheese and fries don't mix."

"No!" Megan said, licking her lips. "We should order onion rings and make them extra crispy!"

Mary's eyes were locked on a food photograph on the menu. "This looks yummy. I say pie for dessert. Apple or blueberry, guys?"

"This chocolate fudge cake looks better!" Nick said, finally looking at his menu.

"And for our drinks, we should all get shakes,"

Samantha suggested. "They're the best."

Megan disagreed. "I don't like shakes. I want orange soda," she said.

"My mom says soda isn't good for you," Mary said. "We should just have milk."

"Wait!" Lyla closed her menu. "Why are we fussing about what to get when we can just get it *all*?"

"Huh?" The Troops looked puzzled.

Lyla discreetly nodded at their cinch sacks and whispered, "We have..."

The Troops still didn't know what Lyla was talking about. "Have what?" Samantha asked.

"This!" Lyla's nodding turned into a direct pointing at her cinch sack.

They were still stumped. "What are you pointing to?" Nick asked.

"The loot!" Lyla shouted. Then she looked around the restaurant to see if anyone had heard her.

"Ohhh, that," the Troops chorused, finally catching on.

Lyla threw up her hands, irritated by their

sudden amnesia. "Yeah, that. Goodness gracious, you guys' memories are horrible! Anyways, we can order *anything* we want on the menu."

"You're right," they all said, smiling.

As they buried their heads back into their menus, the waitress approached their booth to take their order. "What can I get you little people today?" she asked.

Looking down, they saw the waitress's fifteen-inch shoes. From her voice and her peculiar choice of words, they instantly recognized her. "Mrs. Holmes!" they said, shocked. They looked up at the tall figure dressed in an unfashionable Dish Dining uniform. She was wearing an apron and holding a pen and pad.

"Why are *you* working here?" asked Samantha.

"Mayor Crinkle fired me," Mrs. Holmes answered, dropping her head and looking miserable, "when I told him about the Li'berry Fruit."

The Troops felt sorry for her, even if she wasn't one of their biggest fans back then. Sorry to hear that, Mrs. Holmes," Nick said quietly.

"That's OK," she replied. "I left town for a while, and when I returned I was able to get a job working here at Dish Dining. So, where are you little people coming from?"

Samantha turned toward Nick, sitting next to her in the booth, giving him a cutting glance that said, *I know something bad is going to come out of that mouth of yours, so you better be quiet.*

Knowing what Samantha's nonverbal signal meant, Nick turned his head in the opposite direction. He clamped his hand over his mouth and stared out of the window.

"Oh, we're just hanging out," Lyla answered, kicking Mary underneath the table. She hoped that she wouldn't say anything either.

"So what are you little people having today?" Mrs. Holmes asked.

Remembering Lyla's suggestion, the Troops took their turn ordering nearly every food item on the menu. Mrs. Holmes was stunned. As she wrote down their orders, she was dying with curiosity. "Are you sure you little people can pay for all of this?" she asked.

Unable to keep quiet any longer, Nick turned and blurted out, "Of course we can! We're rich!"

Samantha began humming, hoping Mrs. Holmes didn't hear Nick. But she clearly had heard him.

"Oh you are?" Mrs. Holmes said. "And how did you become rich?"

As usual, Lyla stepped in. "We can pay for all of the food because we've been saving up all of our allowance money," she explained. Then she gave Nick a swift kick underneath the table.

"Ouch!" he wailed, bending down and rubbing his shin.

"What happened?" Mrs. Holmes asked, looking at Nick strangely.

"He just hit his knee underneath the table," Samantha said quickly.

"Yeah, these tables can be very short, so be careful," Mrs. Holmes warned. "So, you little people must be getting a lot for your allowance." She was not letting up on the interrogation.

Lyla began to get a bit nervous, but still spoke

for the Troops. "Our parents...have a lot of money?" she said, uncertainly.

Mrs. Holmes became suspicious. But then a couple at table four attracted Mrs. Holmes's attention. "Ma'am, check please," they said, packing up their belongings to leave.

"I'll be back once the cook finishes preparing all of this food." Mrs. Holmes said to the Troops, then turned around and left.

Thankful for the couple at the other table, the Troops sighed a massive sigh of relief. They began arguing with Nick as if no one but them were at the restaurant. Heads at other tables turned at the noise. Even Megan didn't want to stand up for Nick. "You dug your own hole this time," she told him.

"I'm sorry, guys," Nick admitted, feeling bad. "I made a mistake *again*."

Mrs. Holmes soon returned with a smorgasbord of food and drinks, saving him from further bashing. Cheeseburgers were vying to be in the front of the line, wanting to butt aside the colorfully topped pizza. Onion rings tussled with

fries as they lay on the table next to a bowl of hot cheese dipping sauce. Pies begged for a bit of the spotlight, and slices of chocolate truffle cake gleamed with chocolate icing. The shakes were acting cool, but the soda was fizzling with anticipation next to a single glass of milk.

It was like all the food was saying, "Eat me first!"

As soon as Mrs. Holmes sat all the food down on the table, along with some straws, she left to attend to her other customers. The Troops greedily snatched their chosen food and began to devour it like they hadn't eaten in years. Nick stuffed a cheesy slice of pizza down his throat and into his impatient stomach.

"Something smells fishy," Mrs. Holmes mumbled to herself, watching the Troops from afar as she cleared off a table. "And it isn't the catch of the day. I know those little people are up to something and I'm going to get to the bottom of it."

"This food is delectable!" said Lyla, with bits of food between her teeth. The others stared at Lyla. As if reading their minds, Lyla explained, "Delectable is my new word of the day. It means yummy and delicious, as well as delightful and scrumptious, appetizing, tasty...and even lip-smacking."

Whenever she was asked the definition of a word, Lyla became a walking thesaurus. She *loved* spitting out words that had similar meanings. And the Troops were impressed every time. It never grew old with them.

"Those words are like seasoning on my food,"

laughed Nick, pausing with a handful of fries on its way to his mouth.

"Very poetic of you," complemented Lyla.

They giggled as they went on eating.

After everything was cleaned from their plates and the licking of fingers was done, Mrs. Holmes returned. Bursting with curiosity to see how they were going to pay, she slammed the receipt face up in the middle of the table. To her dismay, the owner told her to clean up messy booth eight. Bothered, she rushed off to do her duty, trying to hurry back.

"Let's hurry up and get up out of here before she snoops some more," whispered Lyla, reaching for her cinch sack.

"That's a great idea," Mary said, reaching for a napkin to wipe her mouth.

Samantha grabbed the receipt and began calculating the amount *each* Troop needed to give. "Everyone needs to give forty dollars apiece," she said.

Lyla placed her portion on top of the receipt. Everyone else hastily grabbed their cinch sacks, pulled out a handful of money, and added their money to Lyla's pile.

"How much tip should we give?" Megan asked, taking the receipt from Samantha.

"I think it's fifteen percent of the total amount," Samantha said. "Sooo...that's thirty dollars," she calculated.

They all returned to their cinch sacks and took out five dollars each, except for Lyla. She gave two five-dollar bills. "That should do it," she said, keeping an eye on Mrs. Holmes.

While Mrs. Holmes collected the dirty dishes from booth eight and carried them back to the kitchen, the Troops saw their opportunity to escape. They ran out like the restaurant was on fire, jumped on their bikes and took off like bats, peddling toward Knob Hill as fast as they could.

Mrs. Holmes returned and saw the wad of money on the table. Her eyebrows raised about two inches from their normal height. She was shocked at all the five-dollar bills. She flew out the restaurant, looking for the Troops, and calling to the owner, "I'm taking my lunch break now!"

9

Henry Holmes

Troops ran up the steps to City Hall, eager to tell Mayor Crinkle the *good* news. Once through the double doors, they sped past the few people lingering in the lobby. "Excuse me, ma'am," said Lyla, walking up to the new secretary, Ms. Fanny McGee, who was sitting behind a black desk and writing on a notepad.

Ms. McGee looked up from her notepad and looked at the Troops. "Hello," she greeted them with a welcoming smile. "How may I help you all today?"

"We would like to see Mayor Crinkle," replied Lyla, peering over the top of the desk.

"It's very, very important!" Nick added.

"I'm sorry, but the mayor's out of town at a conference," Ms. McGee said.

Samantha stepped forward and asked, "When is he returning?"

Ms. McGee looked inside the mayor's appointment book on the desk. "He'll be back Saturday," she said.

"Oh no!" The Troops were very disappointed.

Ms. McGee looked concerned. "Is there something I can help you with?"

"No," Lyla said. "*Only* the mayor can help us."

120

"Well, I'll make sure to let him know you all stopped by." Ms. McGee picked up her pen and flipped to a fresh page in her note pad. "What are your names?"

"Lyla Lyte."

"Samantha Huggins."

"Megan Heinz."

"Mary Engelmouth."

"And I'm Nick Nelson."

Ms. McGee added the date and said, "Great!" The phone rang. "OK, you all have a good day." She answered the phone and the Troops walked sadly out.

Outside, Mrs. Holmes finally caught up with them. She was still wearing her apron from Dish Dining. As soon as she saw the Troops walk out of City Hall, she hid around the side of the building.

"Shoot!" said Lyla, as she took a seat on the wide steps. "I wanted to give Mayor Crinkle the loot today. The quicker he gets it, the quicker the library will be built."

The Troops joined her on the steps.

"So, what are we going to do with all of this

loot in our cinch sacks," Megan asked, opening hers and glancing inside.

Did they say loot? Mrs. Holmes thought. *What is that?* It was as if she had supernatural hearing. She stretched her long neck, trying to see inside the cinch sacks.

"Just *take* the loot home and keep it in a safe place," Lyla said. "Until Mayor Crinkle comes back."

"That's a long five days," Nick said, standing up. "I don't think I can control myself."

The more she heard of the Troops' conversation, the more intrigued Mrs. Holmes grew and the more she wanted to find out what they were talking about. "What in the world is loot?" she mumbled to herself.

"Really!" Lyla said as she stood up and faced Nick. "Didn't we talk about this earlier?"

"Yeah, but that was then and this is now," Nick said. "If we were able to give the loot to Mayor Crinkle today, I would have been fine. But, me keeping it inside my house, there's no telling what I would do."

Lyla moved closer to Nick and said, "Hand it over."

"What? My cinch sack?" asked Nick, surprised at Lyla's sudden demand.

"Yes," Lyla answered, sternly.

Nick grasped his sack tightly. "And what am I going to carry my books in?"

Samantha stood and chimed in, "Use one of your mom's huge purses."

They all laughed.

Nick threw his head back. "You have to be kidding!"

"Yeah." Samantha giggled. "My day is not complete unless I mess with you."

"Just carry them in a plastic bag," Mary suggested. "It's only for a few days."

Lyla still had her hand out. "Nick, I'll bring your cinch sack to school in a couple of days. You can't even trust yourself, so give it up!"

Nick released his tight grip and thrust his cinch sack into Lyla's hand. "There!"

"It's for your own good, Nick," Lyla said, grasping the sack and going down the steps. The rest of the Troops tagged behind. Lyla strapped Nick's sack to her bike. She pulled the straps to check the slack to make sure it couldn't fall off while she was riding. "OK, it's secured," she said.

"Is that it, guys?" Megan asked, mounting her bike. "I've got to get home before it gets dark."

"Yup," Lyla said. "I'll see you guys at school tomorrow."

Mrs. Holmes watched the Troops speed off toward their houses. She stepped out from the side of the building and said to herself, "I have to find out what those little rascals are hiding inside of those cinch sacks."

Mrs. Holmes rushed home. Home was a small studio apartment on the second floor of an old run-down building. The living room shared space with the bedroom and the small kitchen was connected to the bathroom. It was cluttered and most of the furniture seemed ancient. She lived with her husband, Henry, who was *not* half as conniving as she was. He had a potbelly and was average height. His head was bald just on the top with a shadow of hair on both sides. He worked as a cashier at Fifty Cents Depot, where everything cost fifty cents and under. When he met her, Mrs. Holmes had told him that she was a billionaire. When they tied the knot, he found out that she didn't even have two dollars in the bank. On top of conning him, she treated him like a puppet.

When she came into the apartment, Mr. Holmes was sitting on the edge of their unmade, twin-size bed, watching sports on their small tubevision. He smiled when his favorite team scored a goal. He was wearing blue jogging pants with elastic at the bottom and a red T-shirt that he always put on after coming home from work.

Mrs. Holmes took the remote control and turned off the tubevision.

"What did you do that for?" he asked, turning to look at his wife.

"Those little rascals are hiding something in their cinch sacks, and I *need* to find out what it is," said Mrs. Holmes.

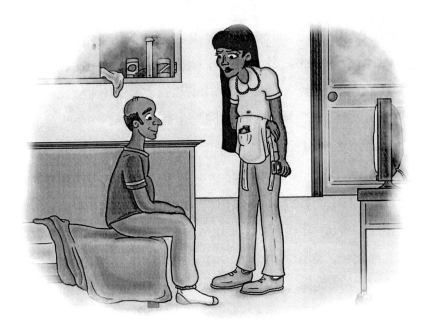

"Who?" he asked, leaping off the bed.

"Lyla Lyte and her little friends, that's who."

"The little girl who grew the Li'berry Fruit?" Mr. Holmes questioned.

"Yes. They came to my restaurant and ordered almost everything on the menu and paid with all five-dollar bills."

"They did?" Mr. Holmes said, taken aback.

"They even gave me this for a tip." She pulled out the money from the pocket of her apron and showed it to her husband.

126

His eyes brightened and his right hand went to touch the money. Mrs. Holmes promptly slapped his hand and pulled the money away. "It's mine, not yours."

She stuffed the money back into her apron before taking it off and throwing it onto the bed. She began pacing back and forth. "I need a way to see what's in those cinch sacks. They call it loot," she said.

"Well, why don't you just ask?" Mr. Holmes suggested, in all innocence.

Mrs. Holmes stopped pacing. "Yeah, I'll just walk up to them and say, 'Show me what you little kids are keeping secret in your cinch sacks,'" she said in a sarcastic voice.

Mr. Holmes shrugged his shoulders. "Well, excuse me."

"Do you know what the word secret means, you nincompoop?" she yelled. Without giving her husband a chance to reply, she continued yelling, "It means they don't want me to find out. But I have news for those little brats. I'm going to expose their little loot secret."

"How?" Mr. Holmes asked. "Sneak in their houses and steal their cinch sacks?" he said, jokingly.

"Hmmm." Mrs. Holmes fell into deep thought.

"You just gave me a splendid idea. Finally you're good for something."

Mr. Holmes ignored that vicious remark about him. "What's the idea?" he asked.

She began explaining, "Mayor Crinkle didn't hire a school principal yet. I can sneak into the school as the new principal and find out their little secret."

"But they know how you look," Mr. Holmes said, eyeing his wife up and down.

"Not if I wear a disguise," she replied and headed for their tall armoire in the corner of the room. She opened it and started flinging outfits out everywhere. The last outfit sitting on the hanger was her husband's green plaid suit. She grabbed it, walked over to the full-length mirror leaning on the wall, and held it in front of her. "A little small, but it will do," she said.

"Are you going as me?" Mr. Holmes asked.

"No," she answered, "but I am going as a man!"

"Only *you* would do that," her husband murmured, not shocked at all at his wife's devious plan.

"Be quiet," Mrs. Holmes said. She had clearly heard his comment. "Go get me that wig you wore when you tried to hide your bald spot—and a pair of scissors and some tape."

She went to the washroom, and Mr. Holmes went to retrieve the items his daring wife had requested.

Mrs. Holmes shaved off a thin strip of the wig. She put on the suit that was obviously too tight, tucked her hair underneath the wig, and taped the mustache to her top lip. She looked in the mirror and said, "Perfect!"

Lyla Lyte and the Loot Tree

10

The New Principal

Right before the start of school, Mrs. Holmes found the window to the principal's office unlocked. She pried it open, snuck inside, and sat behind the mahogany desk while Mr. Holmes waited in their little Volkswagen Beetle, unseen, around the corner.

As soon as Ms. Verdak began class, she was interrupted by an unfamiliar voice over the intercom. "Sorry to bother you, Ms. Verdak," Mrs. Holmes said in a deep, croaky, disguised voice.

"No problem," replied Ms. Verdak. She was just about to dive into integers.

"My name is..." Mrs. Holmes paused, looking around the desk for *anything* to give her an idea for a last name. The desk lamp caught her eye. "...Principal Lampert. I'm the new principal of Crinkle Academy," Mrs. Holmes proclaimed.

Ms. Verdak was surprised. There had been no formal introduction of the new principal, but she had seen stranger things happen in Coverfield. "Nice to meet you...I mean speak to you, sir," she acknowledged, projecting her voice into the intercom speaker mounted high up on the classroom wall.

"Thank you," Mrs. Holmes responded, dropping her voice deeper. "I would like you to please send the Troops...Oops! I mean Lyla, Samantha, Megan, Nick, and Mary down to the office with their cinch sacks," she said.

"OK," Ms. Verdak said. She sat down at her desk and retrieved a blank hall pass.

"What does he need to see us for?" asked Lyla, looking at the other Troops. They all shrugged their shoulders, wondering why as well.

"Are we getting suspended?" Nick asked, worried. "And I don't have my cinch sack."

Everyone walked slowly toward Ms. Verdak's desk.

Ms. Verdak wrote their names on the hall pass and gave it to them to carry. Then they proceeded nervously to the office. There was little talk among the Troops during the slow walk down the hallway. When they arrived at the principal's office, they each took a deep breath, and Lyla knocked on the door.

"Come in little students," Mrs. Holmes called out.

The Troops entered hesitantly, with Lyla in front of the line.

Mrs. Holmes told them to take a seat in the four chairs in front of her desk. They placed their cinch sacks in the corner and sat down with two of them sharing a seat.

"Hi, Principal Lampert," they said in unison, with pleasant voices. "Welcome to our school."

"Thank you," Mrs. Holmes said. Then she began to explain why she called them to the office. "In hiring me as the new principal of Crinkle Academy, Mayor Crinkle wants to make sure that I'm providing the best education for our students. In order for me to that, I want to get to know each of you all as much as I can."

Samantha hurriedly raised her hand, "Excuse me, Principal Lampert."

"Yes," said Mrs. Holmes.

"You look kind of like this lady we know called Mrs. Holmes," Samantha said, looking closely at the new principal's physical features.

"Is she your sister?" Lyla asked. She had noticed the similarities as well. "Because you sound like her too."

"No, never heard her name before," Mrs. Holmes said, making sure not to blow her cover. "Who is she?"

"Someone who used to work for Mayor Crinkle and now she works at Dish Dinning," Megan answered.

Nick pointed to Mrs. Holmes's face. "Ummm, Mr. Lampert, your mustache."

Mrs. Holmes grabbed the gray hand-held mirror that was lying on the desk. What stared back at her? A mustache that was tilted at an odd angle. *This is not good!* she thought. "You can't find a good barber these days," she said as she straightened her mustache.

"The new principal is weird," Mary whispered to Megan.

"You're right," she whispered back.

"I'm aware that you were the ones that found the strange seed that grew the books," Mrs. Holmes said as she put down the mirror and adjusted her mustache with one last tilt.

"Yeah, that was us," Lyla said.

"Well, I'm very proud of you all that you got *everyone* reading in Coverfield." Mrs. Holmes held up a book that also sat on the desk. "Later this year, we are going to have a celebration for you all."

The Troops were buying into Mrs. Holmes's lie. They became extremely excited and were grinning from ear to ear.

"Is there going to be pizza?" Nick asked. Once again, his mind was on food.

"Anything you all want," answered Mrs. Holmes, spreading her arms wide.

The Troops jumped out of their seats and cheered.

"Wait," Mrs. Holmes interrupted, stopping the premature celebration. "Right now there is something more important than your pizza party."

"What?" The Troops plopped back down in their seats.

Mrs. Homes explained, "As you know, the mayor is faced with a financial crisis. He is unable to raise the money to build the library, so we need everyone in Coverfield to help out." She pointed to the Troops. "That even means our students. Just like you all solved the book problem in Coverfield, I need you to come up with a solution to help Mayor Crinkle. He really needs your help, so don't let him down."

The Troops hunched over and began whispering among themselves. Mrs. Holmes was curious about what they could be discussing and she tried to read their lips. When their talk came to a close, Lyla looked at Mrs. Holmes and confidently said, "We can help."

"How?" Mrs. Holmes asked. She was excited and her voice became high-pitched. Remembering that she was supposed to be a man, she cleared her throat and adjusted her voice again. "I mean how can you kids help?" she said with a deep growl in her voice.

"Well, we went to see Mayor Crinkle yesterday to give him something, but his secretary told us that he was at a conference," Lyla explained.

"What were you kids going to give him?" Mrs.

Holmes asked, looking at the cinch sacks.

"We grew a Loot Tree," Lyla said with excitement.

Mrs. Holmes was baffled. "You grew a what tree?"

"A money tree!" Lyla answered.

"Did I hear you correctly?" Mrs. Holmes stood up.

"Yes," Mary said, nodding her head in confirmation.

"That's amazing!" Mrs. Holmes exclaimed as goose bumps popped all over her arms. *How dumb of me*, she thought. *Loot is a synonym for money. These little people are smarter than I thought.* She couldn't control her excitement. "So, open up your cinch sacks," she said, pointing to them in the corner.

"For what?" Nick asked, puzzled by Mrs. Holmes odd request.

"Just open them," said Mrs. Holmes, anxious to see all of the money.

The Troops got their cinch sacks and poured the contents out on the principal's desk. It was

nothing but books and school supplies inside.

"Where is the loot?" Mrs. Holmes asked, stunned. "And why are there only four cinch sacks?"

"We left all the loot at our houses," Lyla answered.

"I don't have my cinch sack," Nick added warily, as the principal was becoming aggravated. "Lyla has it."

"How did you know we had carried the loot in our cinch sacks?" Lyla asked, trying to remember if they told the principal.

"Well...you said you were going to give Mayor Crinkle something, so I assumed you had it in your cinch sacks," Mrs. Holmes explained. Then waited to see how they responded to her lie.

The Troops bought into her fib again. "OK," they said.

Mrs. Holmes needed more information. She needed to know where the Loot Tree was located. "Words can't explain how exceedingly proud I am of all of you, and I know the mayor will be as well. You kids are very brave."

They all smiled, swollen with pride.

Mrs. Holmes continued grilling them. "So where did you grow this Loot Tree?"

"The dumpsite," said Samantha.

"That nasty, polluted place!" Mrs. Holmes screeched. She thought of a way to keep them from going back. "I do *not* want you all returning to that place again. It's filled with life-threatening germs and bacteria. And if you do, I will be forced to suspend all of you!"

"But that's where the money is for Mayor

Crinkle," Lyla said.

Nick pulled on Lyla's pants. "My mom will kill me if I get suspended," he squealed.

"When Mayor Crinkle returns, I will make sure he is told about the Loot Tree. You little people have done enough. Now it's time to go back to your classes." Mrs. Holmes began pushing them out of the door. "Now remember," she said in a low voice, placing her long finger across her lips, "the Loot Tree is our little secret."

"They grew a money tree," Mrs. Holmes bellowed excitingly as she jumped into the passenger seat of the Beetle. Her wig was falling off her head and her fake mustache tumbled to her chin where it looked like she had grown a goatee.

A money tree?" Mr. Holmes repeated. His chest was touching the steering wheel. He always pulled his seat as close as possible when he drove. "Where?" he asked, just as amped as his wife.

"Drive, drive!" Mrs. Holmes shouted, pulling

off her wig and mustache and throwing them in the back seat. "It's in the town's dumpsite."

A happy Mr. Holmes drove rapidly away and in no time the Beetle was parked at the entrance to the dumpsite. They were instantly disgusted by the sight of garbage everywhere.

"Yuck!" Mrs. Holmes exclaimed, looking out of the car window.

"It's such a filthy and mucky place," Mr. Holmes said, wrinkling his nose like he could smell the stench from inside the car. "I'll stay in here and watch the car while you look for the money tree inside.

Mrs. Holmes yanked her husband by the right ear. "Henry Holmes you are following me everywhere I go."

"Ouch!" he screeched as he tried to pull away, but her grip became tighter. "I'm coming!" he said.

She let go and he jumped out and ran to the other side of the car to open the door for his wife. No matter how badly she treated him, he was always a gentleman.

"We need something to put the money in," said Mrs. Holmes as soon as she got out.

Mr. Holmes rummaged through the trunk. "What about this?" he asked, holding up some hefty garbage bags.

"That should work," Mrs. Holmes said. She waved her hand in the direction of the entrance. "Follow *me!*"

"I'm right behind you, dear," Mr. Holmes said, hurrying after his wife.

Avoiding piles of garbage and unknown chemicals, Mrs. Holmes walked through the dumpsite in the men's dress shoes she had worn to match her disguise.

Mr. Holmes squished garbage under his feet as he tried tiptoeing. "Disgusting, filthy!" he exclaimed squeezing his nose.

"Where is that Loot Tree!" yelled a frustrated Mrs. Holmes. "It should be here somewhere!"

"We'll find it," Mr. Holmes said, encouraging his wife in order to calm her down.

"I *need* that money," she said, her eyes bouncing in every direction.

They both searched the dumpsite up and down for what seemed like hours but still had no luck.

"I'm tired," Mr. Holmes said. He was sweating through his shirt and decided to take a break from searching. He stood on one foot, lifted the other and started rubbing his ankle. He felt a sharp pain in his feet.

"There's no time to rest," Mrs. Holmes barked.

Mr. Holmes cried out with an anguished look on his face. "But, my feet hurt!"

"I said *keep* looking!" Mrs. Holmes shouted, releasing all of the air from her lungs.

Mr. Holmes was startled and fell backward over a pile of garbage, rolling a few feet away. When he stood, there was the Loot Tree. "Oh my!" he cried.

Still yelling, Mrs. Holmes let her husband have it with a barrage of questions, as she marched toward him. "How can you be so clumsy? Why did I marry you? What are you good for?"

Mr. Holmes was motionless with his eyes locked on the Loot Tree.

"Are you just going to stand there like a statue and say nothing to defend yourself?" Mrs. Holmes asked. "Henry Holmes, look at me when I talk you!" she commanded, wearing her angriest face.

Mr. Holmes was still in a daze.

"What is wrong with you?" she squawked as she reached her husband.

He extended his left arm and pointed in the direction of the Loot Tree.

Mrs. Holmes turned her head and stopped in awe as she saw the tree of money. "Do you see that; do you see that?" she said, shaking her husband.

"Yes, yes," he replied, finally able to speak.

"I'm going to be wealthy!" she cried. She sprinted to the Loot Tree, and, as she was almost as tall as it, she easily started plucking money off the branches. "Bring the garbage bags over here," she ordered, "and start collecting money!"

The garbage bags were bloated in no time. Then they began filling up their pockets. "Thanks to those little brats, I'll be able to teach Mayor Crinkle a lesson for firing me!" Mrs. Holmes said.

"And what is that, my dear?" asked Mr. Holmes.

"I'm going to run against that awful mayor in the election," Mrs. Holmes announced with an evil smirk, squeezing a hand full of money.

Mr. Holmes was flabbergasted by his wife's self-nomination. "You're going to do what?" he asked, taking a break from stuffing his pockets.

"I'm going to be the *next* Mayor of Coverfield!" Mrs. Holmes declared.

11

Vote

"Dad, look." Lyla pointed to an 18 × 24 white poster stapled on the oak tree in their front yard. It had caught her eye as her dad was backing out of the garage to take her to school.

Mr. Lyte stopped the family van in the driveway. "It looks like an advertisement of some sort," he said, surprised as well.

"Who put it there?" Lyla asked, peering out of the van's window that had been imprinted with drawings from Joey's sticky fingers.

"I don't know," her dad answered, shrugging his shoulders. "Go get it," he said, putting the van in park.

Lyla jumped out and snatched the poster from

the tree, ripping the corners on the staples.

"What does it say?" asked Mr. Lyte, turning around.

Lyla examined the poster and read the heading aloud, "Vote For Me And Receive Five Dollars" it said, in bold, black letters.

"Vote for *who*?" her dad asked, scrunching up his eyebrows.

Lyla read on. "Mrs. Holmes. It says she's running for mayor of Coverfield." Mrs. Holmes's cheesy face was plastered across the middle of the poster.

"For mayor?" Mr. Lyte repeated. He was in shock. He held out his hand. "Let me see that." He took the poster from Lyla and looked down at it. "You're right!" he said. "At five o'clock today she's having a rally at Program Park. This will be the first time someone goes up against Mayor Crinkle."

After hearing the word *rally*, Lyla immediately wanted to look it up. She retrieved her pocket dictionary and searched for the word. "Can she do that?" she asked her dad.

"Run for mayor?"

"No," Lyla said. "Can she buy people's votes?"

Mr. Lyte turned back toward Lyla and said, "I don't know if she can or not. That's something Mayor Crinkle would have to answer."

"If she can, that's not good for Mayor Crinkle," said Lyla.

However, her dad was less partial. "I'm sure if Mrs. Holmes became mayor, she will do a fine job as well," he commented.

In Lyla's mind Mayor Crinkle was the gateway to the new library and she was stuck on the possibility of Mayor Crinkle loosing. "We don't know what type of mayor Mrs. Holmes would be. Mayor Crinkle wants to build the library. Mrs. Holmes might not want to," she said.

"I think you're thinking way too far into the future," Mr. Lyte said. "She still needs a majority of the votes to win the election."

"Well, I'm not voting for her!" Lyla stated, squeezing her little fist.

Her dad chuckled. "You *can't* vote."

"Why not?" Lyla asked, disappointed.

Her dad put the poster on the passenger seat and looked at Lyla, he stretched out his hands with his palms facing outward and fingers spread wide on one hand. He bent his thumb inward on the other one. "You're only nine years old." He showed her. "You need to be eighteen or older."

"That sucks!" Lyla said, crinkling up the corner of her lips.

"Well, laws are made to be followed," Mr. Lyte replied. "You only have to wait nine more years to exercise your right to vote."

Lyla did not find that amusing at all. "Dad, that's a long time!"

"The years will go by quicker than you think," he said, in a fatherly way. "Just yesterday, it seems as though you were Joey's age, and we were changing your diapers."

"Hopefully, my diapers weren't as smelly as his," Lyla said, waving her hand in front of her nose. "Because Dentapotamus's diapers smell like a skunk on diarrhea."

"Yeah, he can lay a stink bomb at times," her dad said.

"Are you gonna vote for Mrs. Holmes?" asked Lyla, curious about which side her dad was leaning toward.

"Well..." her dad paused and thought for a few seconds. "I would be able to buy myself a *five-dollar foot-long*," he said with a smirk on his face.

"Dad, pleassse...don't vote for her," Lyla begged, clasping her hands as if she was praying. "She's just too nosy!"

Mr. Lyte couldn't deny that. "She sure is! But don't worry. I'll vote for Mayor Crinkle," he assured her.

Lyla's smile bounced back. "And make sure Mommy does too," she said.

"I'll make sure," he replied. "Let's just hope the majority of Coverfield feels the same way."

They have to, thought Lyla.

"So did you find that word you were looking for?" her dad asked, turning to look at her dictionary.

"Oh yeah...I completely forgot." Lyla said. She still had the dictionary opened with her thumb on the word *perpendicular* instead of *rally*. She resumed her search, found the definition, and read it aloud, "Rally means to gather people together for a common cause."

Lyla's dad nodded his head, indicating that was it.

"So who are the people that will attend her rally?" Lyla asked, closing her dictionary.

"Anyone who supports Mrs. Holmes and wants to hear what she has to say."

"With any luck it's just Mr. and Mrs. Holmes." Lyla said, crossing her fingers.

"I would assume there would be more people than just those two," her dad said. "But kudos to you for wishful thinking."

Where is a falling star when I need it? Lyla thought.

"OK, it's time to go," Mr. Lyte announced, putting his hands back on the steering wheel. He put the car in reverse and finished backing out of the driveway. All the trees, light posts, and traffic light posts in Coverfield had posters attached to them. Lyla grew more worried.

During recess after Language Arts, the Troops headed to their meeting spot. They had all noticed the posters on their way to school.

"Those stupid posters are all over Coverfield," Lyla said. "It's going to be tough for Mayor Crinkle to win if Mrs. Holmes is paying everyone five dollars to vote for her!"

Samantha began counting numbers in her

head. "About how many adult citizens are there in Coverfield?" she inquired.

"Probably forty thousand," Lyla guessed, throwing out a high number.

"If everyone voted for Mrs. Holmes," Samantha said. "She will have to give away a total of two hundred thousand dollars."

"Whoaaa!" Nick exclaimed with big bubble eyes. "Mrs. Holmes must be rich!"

Lyla was skeptical. "Then why is she working at Dish Dining? If she was wealthy, she would own it."

"Yeah," agreed Mary. "She wouldn't be driving that itty bitty car, either."

"So where is she getting all this money from to pay people to vote for her?" Megan was also tremendously curious.

Samantha added her thought into the thinking pot, which was already bubbling with curiosity. "Why didn't she tell us that she was running for mayor when we ate at the restaurant?"

"Maybe she worked overtime," Nick assumed,

giving Mrs. Holmes the benefit of the doubt.

Lyla contested that idea. "So in two days Mrs. Holmes earned enough money from working at a sucky job to pay for the whole town of Coverfield to vote for her." She looked at Nick. "Really, you believe that?"

"Well excuse me for thinking of other possibilities," Nick said.

Megan pointed to all of them, then to herself, and said, "We made a lot of money overnight."

"From scratch," Nick added, smiling. "Like us, Mrs. Holmes is a fiveionare!"

"Wait a minute...five dollars!" Lyla said. Then she fell into deep thought. "Troops, I think we've been bamboozled!" she yelled out.

"Bam-who-zled?" said Nick. He was hearing the foreign-sounding word for the first time.

Lyla expounded, throwing out every synonym that popped into her head. "We've been deceived, swindled, flimflammed, mislead, duped, hood-winked, outwitted, swindled, fooled, and tricked!"

The Troops were baffled. "Tricked!"

"What do you mean?" Megan asked.

Lyla went on, "Isn't it weird that Principal Lampert looks a lot like Mrs. Holmes?"

"Yeah, but they say everyone looks like someone else in the world," Nick said. "They say I look like Kobe Bryant!"

Samantha giggled. "If they did, *you've* been hoodwinked."

"Seriously, guys," Lyla said trying to keep everyone focused on her theory. "When we see Principal Lampert today, take a good look at him...or her."

"He's not here today," Mary said.

"How do you know that?" Lyla asked.

"I told my mom we had a new principal, and she wanted to meet him. She went to the office this morning and it was closed," Mary replied.

Lyla became more excited as she continued to prove her point. "Don't you guys think that's odd? Our new principal's first day was yesterday, and he's already absent."

Samantha began to digest Lyla's idea. "So you're saying Principal Lampert is really Mrs. Holmes?"

"Yes!" Lyla said. "Someone finally gets my point."

Nick stroked his bare top lip. "But Principal Lampert has a mustache,"

"A mustache that was falling off his, I mean her, face," Lyla exclaimed. "That was no bad haircut; that was a bad fake mustache, and now that I think about it more, that was probably a wig she had on!"

As the other Troops gave it more thought, they started to come around to Lyla's theory.

"You might be right," Megan said. "Out of all of the students, she only called us to come to the office."

"And she asked to look into our cinch sacks." Lyla remembered the strange request.

"She thought we still had the loot in there," Samantha added.

It finally sunk into their heads that Mrs. Holmes had pulled a hoax on them.

"Oh no!" Mary cried, covering her mouth with her hand. "We told her about the Loot Tree!"

"And where it's located," added Nick, shaking his head.

"We *need* to go back to the dump site after school," Lyla said.

12

All Gone

When they arrived, the Troops wasted no time in finding the Loot Tree. To their dismay, they found they were right.

"*All* the loot is gone from the tree!" Lyla yelped, distraught.

"You were right," Megan said, looking at Lyla's gloomy expression.

Nick stared at the bare branches. "Mrs. Holmes took every last five-dollar bill."

Lyla crossed her arms, grunting, "Guaranteed she'll be back tomorrow morning to feed her appetite!"

"What should we do?" Samantha asked.

"I think it's time we told our parents," Mary

said.

The Troops considered the suggestion for a while and eventually they agreed.

"I guess you're right," Lyla said. "Maybe our parents can put a stop to Mrs. Holmes's..." She paused, pulled out her pocket dictionary, and quickly flipped through the words to find the one she had previously read in a book, "...*diabolical* plan!" she said aloud.

"Guys, look at this." said Nick, who was kneeling down and wearing a funny-looking, brown, old-fashioned hat that he had pulled from his cinch sack, which Lyla had returned to him that morning. He took out a black-framed magnifying lens and started examining the ground.

"What are you wearing?" Samantha asked in bewilderment. "And what do you have in your hand?"

"It's a hat just like Sherlock Holmes would wear," Nick responded matter-of-factly. He was deeply focused on what he was looking at. "And this is a magnifying lens. I'm looking for clues just like Sherlock Holmes would do at a crime scene."

"Sherlock Holmes?" Samantha asked, stumped.

Nick explained, "Yeah, I'm reading *The Adventures of Sherlock Holmes.*"

"Why are you reading about Mrs. Holmes's husband?" Mary questioned.

"Yeah, Nick?" Lyla was also curious. She gave him a look like he was a traitor. "Why are you reading about Mrs. Holmes's husband? I thought you were into superheroes."

Nick laughed. "He's not Mrs. Holmes's

husband. He's the greatest detective ever." Out of all of the Troops, Nick had the biggest imagination. He always found himself pretending to be the fictional character he was reading about. Nick brushed the loose pebbles away from the spot he was examining. "These footprints belong to Mrs. Holmes." They were so large both of Nick's feet could fit in one print with ease.

I could have told you that," Samantha remarked, in a smart-alecky way.

"If you had let me finish," Nick said, glaring up at Samantha from underneath his hat, "you would have heard me say that there are two set of footprints."

"There are?" The girls exclaimed. They were astounded and impressed by Nick's detective skills.

He explained further, pointing at the ground. "These foot prints are a little smaller than Mrs. Holmes. And if you look closer, the person must have been dragging some heavy bags."

Mary crouched to look at what Nick was examining. "How do you know that?"

"There are long drag marks in the soil." Nick pointed them out to the others.

They inspected further. "Nick you're right," they all said.

"The other crook was probably carrying bags full of *our* money," Nick added as he stood and pointed to the drag marks trailing the footprints.

"Who do you think it is?" asked Lyla.

"It had to be her husband," Nick replied confidently. "He's the only one that would help her with her *di-a-bol-i-cal* plan."

Lyla was shocked. "Nick, you used one of my new words, and you pronounced it correctly."

"Yes indeed," Nick said as he tipped his hat.

Lyla glanced at her watch and said, "Mrs. Holmes's rally should be starting in thirty minutes. We should go to hear the other lies she's telling people to get their votes."

"Well, let's get moving, then" said Nick, removing his hat and throwing it and the magnifying lens back into his cinch sack.

The Troops mounted their bikes once more and rode off to Program Park.

When they got to the park, the Troops saw that a nice size crowd had gathered. The townspeople chattered among themselves, discussing their shock at hearing that Mrs. Holmes was going to be a candidate. They were all curious to see if they would really receive five dollars for voting for her. The Troops were anxious not to be seen, so they stayed at the back of the crowd.

Mr. Holmes had set up a brown, wooden podium and a portable microphone system with two huge speakers sitting on the side. On the podium was a rectangle banner with an image of Mrs. Holmes waving money in her hand. The caption read "Five Dollars Per Vote."

Mrs. Holmes approached the podium and banged her hand over the microphone, which made a loud screeching, echoing sound. It caught everyone's attention and gradually the noise died down. "Hello, people of Coverfield," Mrs. Holmes began, looking out into the sea of faces. "My name is Patricia Lillian Holmes, and I'm running to be the next Mayor of Coverfield."

Mr. Holmes held a sign up high that read in capital letters, "CLAP." The crowd obeyed and cheered.

Mrs. Holmes continued, "I'm glad to see all of you beautiful people out here today to support me."

"They're here because you stole our money," Lyla said angrily to herself.

Mr. Holmes flipped the sign over, and it read, "Chant, Mrs. Holmes for mayor."

Once again the crowd obeyed and chanted, "Mrs. Holmes for Mayor!"

"Look at them. They're like her *minions*. She's telling them what to say and when to say it. This is just pathetic," said Samantha with a groan.

"This town needs a new leader!" Mrs. Holmes declared, pointing to herself with her thumb. "And I'm the best person for the job."

The crowd clapped as Mr. Holmes flipped the sign.

Mrs. Holmes snatched the microphone from the stand and left the podium. She walked directly to the edge of the stage, gave the crowd a serious look, and cried, "Don't you want change?"

A crowd member shouted, "No, I want dollar bills for my vote!"

"I'll gladly take change," someone else said. "Quarters, nickels, dimes. I'll even take pennies."

"Not that type of change," Mrs. Holmes said, a little annoyed by their misunderstanding. She made the question clearer. "I mean change as in a

166

new mayor for Coverfield."

"Is Mayor Crinkle giving five dollars for his vote?" a lady in the crowd asked.

Mrs. Holmes shook her head back and forth. "No! I'm the only one."

"In that case, you have my vote," the lady bellowed, as she pumped her fist in the air.

"And mine!"

"Mine too!"

"Can we vote today?"

There was a rush of excitement among the crowd.

Mr. Holmes turned the volume up on the audio system and played music in the background. Mrs. Holmes began throwing one hand in the air with her fingers spread apart, bouncing, and instructed the audience, "I say five dollars...you say vote."

She shouted. "Five dollars!"

"Vote!" they screamed.

"Five dollars!"

"Vote!"

The crowd went wild. Mrs. Holmes made them

go even more bananas.

Being the dancer she was, Megan started grooving with the crowd. It was as if she had been hypnotized and had forgotten she was anti-Mrs. Holmes. She appeared to be in a trance.

"Megan!" the Troops called out her name.

"Vote!" Megan started to shout along with the crowd, pumping her fists in the air as well.

The Troops called again, louder. "Megan!"

She was *just* about to bust out her hip-hop moves when Lyla went up to her and lightly whacked her in the head. "Megan, do you realize what you are doing?" she asked.

Megan, finally snapped out of her dancing trance, realized what she was doing, and stopped. "I'm sorry, guys." She felt ashamed. "I don't know what got into me. I just heard music and started boogying."

"As long as you're back on our side, no problem," Nick said with relief.

Just then, Mrs. Holmes began walking through the crowd, shaking hands and kissing babies, while Mr. Holmes was passing out blue vote buttons with pictures of Mrs. Holmes and her slogan.

"OK, Troops. Let's get out of here, before Mrs. Holmes catches *us*," said Lyla.

They made their way through the cheering crowd, got on their bikes, and left for home.

13

Underneath Lyla's Mattress

When Lyla arrived home, both her parents, along with Dentapotamus, were waiting in the living room for her. Mr. and Mrs. Lyte were sitting down on one side of the couch while Dentapotamus was sitting on the carpet and making the sound of a sheep, "Baaa, Baaa!" he read, following along in his children's picture book, *Where Are the Animals?*

"Hi, Mom and Dad," Lyla said, coming in from the garage where she had parked her bike.

"Sit down, young lady," Mr. Lyte ordered, sternly.

Her dad's look meant that she was in serious trouble. She cautiously took a seat on the other side of the couch and racked her brain trying to figure out what she could have done wrong.

Her dad grabbed a pillowcase from the carpet and poured its contents on to the coffee table. Five-dollar bills scattered all over the table top, nearly covering it.

Lyla sat there stunned that they had found the loot.

Dentapotomous dropped his book and went up to the coffee table and began playing with the money. He started flinging it everywhere.

"When your mom was cleaning your room," Mr. Lyte began, sounding angry, "she found this money stuffed underneath your mattress and she put it in this pillow case. Where did you get all this money from?" he asked.

Lyla glanced at her mom with worried eyes and tried to avoid her dad's.

"Lyla you *can* tell the truth," her mom said with a less harsh voice, but it was clear that she was angry too.

"I was going to tell you," said Lyla, fretfully. "We grew a Loot Tree."

"You grew a what?" Mr. Lyte asked.

"A Loot Tree," Lyla repeated, turning to face her dad.

Lyla's dad was shocked. "You mean loot as in money?" he asked, standing up.

She nodded, "Yeah!"

Lyla's mom got up and walked over to the pile of money and grabbed a handful. "You grew this?" she asked with widened eyes.

"Yeah." Lyla said again, cautiously, as she walked over to the other side of the coffee table.

"Thank, goodness!" Mrs. Lyte exclaimed, throwing the money back onto the coffee table and giving her daughter a comforting hug, knocking down her husband onto the couch.

Mr. Lyte was baffled. "Why are you hugging her?" he asked. "She literally grew a money tree without our permission!"

Mrs. Lyte explained, beaming, "I thought *she* had robbed a bank!"

"A bank? Now that's just silly," commented Mr. Lyte, making Lyla chuckle.

173

"What else was I supposed to think when I found this heap of money?" Mrs. Lyte said, removing Lyla from her hug.

"Anything but our daughter being a bank robber," Mr. Lyte said, laughing a little as well.

"We're getting off topic," Mrs. Lyte said, shifting into a mix of relief and anger. "Back to you, young lady! Who helped you grow this so called Loot Tree?" she asked, making her two fingers on both hands into bunny ears and bending them up and down to make air quotes.

"The Troops," said Lyla.

Her dad looked stern. "How?"

Lyla explained. "We used the sap from the Li'berry Tree and buried it with a five-dollar bill that Nick gave us."

"Did you grow the Loot Tree in our backyard?" Mr. Lyte asked, running to the kitchen and parting the window curtains.

"No!" Lyla said.

"Then, where?" her mom and dad asked together.

Lyla hesitated and lowered her head once

more. She muttered in a low voice, "At the dump site."

Her mom really became upset with her. "Didn't I tell you *never* to go back to that place again?"

Hoping the reason would outweigh her disobedience, Lyla said, "I know, Mom, but we really wanted to help Mayor Crinkle raise money to build the library."

"Lyla, you have *good* intentions, but putting yourself and your friends in danger is no excuse," her dad said.

"I'm sorry, but Ms. Verdak taught us about DNA, and we wanted to see if a tree could grow like the Li'berry Fruit...but instead of books...money."

"How much money did you all actually grow?" her dad questioned.

"A lot!" Lyla exclaimed, spreading her arms wide.

Her dad's mood suddenly changed. "I'll be right back." He hurried off to the garage. Lyla and Mrs. Lyte heard a lot of ruckus going on. Auto parts and tools falling on the floor. The van door opening and slamming. Finally, they heard Mr. Lyte shout, "Found it!" He ran back into the living room.

"What was all of that noise for?" Mrs. Lyte asked.

"I was looking for this," Mr. Lyte answered as he showed them an issue of American Mechanic Catalog. He opened it to page twenty-four and showed them a Car Lifting System. "I've been needing this lift for the longest time," he said.

Lyla realized what her dad was implying. "Dad, the money on the tree is for the new library," she said. It was as if a role reversal had occurred. Lyla was like the parent telling her dad he couldn't buy his expensive toy!

"Just this one time, pleeease," Mr. Lyte begged, desperately.

Mrs. Lyte stared at her husband with disappointed eyes and said, "That's enough Michael. You're setting a bad example for our daughter."

"Shoot!" Mr. Lyte pouted, closing the

magazine.

"Dad, you were right," said Lyla.

"About what?"

"Money makes people crazy!" Lyla said.

"You mean people like your father?" her mom asked, pointing at him.

"Kinda," Lyla responded. "But I'm really talking about Mrs. Holmes. She found out about the Loot Tree, then tricked us and stole all of the money from it."

"OK, on her behalf she was always a little crazy," Lyla's dad said, pointing his right pointing finger at his forehead and swirling it around.

"The money made her even crazier," Lyla said, her eyes huge. "When she found out about the Loot Tree, she decided to use the money to buy *everyone's* vote."

"So that's where she's getting the money from," said Mr. Lyte, remembering what he had read on the poster.

"We just came from the rally, and everyone is saying they're going to vote for her," Lyla explained.

"Who else knows about the Loot Tree?" her dad asked.

Lyla pointed to herself. "Just me and the Troops."

"What about Mayor Crinkle?" her mom asked.

"No. We went to tell him but he was out of town at a conference," Lyla said, sounding distressed.

"When will he be back?" her mom asked.

"This weekend," Lyla replied. "We need to put a stop to Mrs. Holmes before he returns." She pounded her fist in the palm of her other hand.

"Lyla, we do not have the power to do that. It's best to wait for Mayor Crinkle to come back and let him deal with her." Her dad looked regretful.

"Then, it's going to be too late," Lyla said, looking troubled.

14

The Flyer

Saturday, Mayor Crinkle returned from his conference. He was curious to see how his town had fared while he was away. While zooming passed Gooblers Groceries, a flyer in the window caught his attention. "Mr. Butler, did you see what that flyer just said?" he asked.

"No, it's probably someone trying to find their missing dog." Mr. Butler responded.

"It sure looked like a person's face instead of a dog's face."

After driving for a few more minutes, a flyer flew by in the wind, passing the limo window. Before Mayor Crinkle could make out Mrs. Holmes's face, the wind flipped the flyer over so

the blank side was up. "See, *there's* some more!" he said, with a hint of frustration in his voice. He usually didn't see flyers scattered all around Coverfield.

"Sir, don't you think you're overreacting a bit?" said Mr. Butler, keeping his eyes glued on the road.

"I'm not overreacting!" Mayor Crinkle refuted.

About two streets later, Mr. Butler stopped at a red light. On the traffic light pole by Ellis Street was a flyer. Before the light switched to green,

Mayor Crinkle rolled down his window, stretched out his hand, and snatched the flyer.

"Got it!" he shouted happily.

"Got what?" Mr. Butler asked.

"The flyer," Mayor Crinkle answered, rolling up his window. "It's my responsibility to know what's going on in my town." He looked at it. "Why's she on here?" He muttered, confused. Then he read on and froze.

Mr. Butler looked into the rear view mirror and saw that Mayor Crinkle was motionless. "What's wrong, sir?" he inquired, concerned.

"She's running for mayor!" He cried out.

The mayor's sudden outburst startled Mr. Butler causing him to lose control of the limo. They veered into the other lane. "Honk, honk!" The driver of the oncoming car blew his horn. Regaining control, Mr. Butler swerved back to his lane. "That was close," he said, a little frightened.

"I can't believe she has the audacity to run against me," Mayor Crinkle said.

"Who's running for mayor?" Mr. Butler asked, stepping on the brakes to slow down.

"Mrs. Holmes."

"Isn't she that tall...very, very tall lady you fired a long time ago?" Mr. Butler asked.

Mayor Crinkle looked worried. "Yes, it seems she has decided to run against me for mayor." His voice trailed off. "And it says here that she's giving away five dollars for each vote!"

"She's going to be tough to beat," said Mr. Butler.

"She has *no* political experience, and anyway the best person for the job will prevail!" Mayor Crinkle believed it, wholeheartedly.

As they neared City Hall, they couldn't ride a block without seeing Mrs. Holmes face plastered somewhere. "My town is flooded with these ridiculous things!" the mayor complained.

"We're here, sir," Mr. Butler announced when they pulled up at City Hall.

"I leave for a few days, and I return to this!" Mayor Crinkle grumbled as he got out, entered City Hall, and trotted down the lobby to get to the front desk where his secretary, Ms. McGee, was sitting. "Am I crazy or is Mrs. Holmes running for mayor?" he asked, showing her the flyer. "And please tell me I'm going delusional."

Ms. McGee looked up at Mayor Crinkle and replied, "Actually, sir, you're not crazy. She is running to be the next mayor of Coverfield,"

"This is absurd!" Mayor Crinkle exclaimed, turning red. "She's probably just running to get back at me for firing her."

"Sorry you're not having a good morning, sir," Ms. McGee said.

"I'm not going to let this ruin my day," Mayor Crinkle said, balling up the flyer and throwing it into the wastebasket next to Ms. McGee's desk. "I have a town to run."

An hour later, Ms. McGee called the mayor on his phone.

Mayor Crinkle picked up, "Yes, Ms. McGee."

"The Lytes are here to speak to you, sir," Ms. McGee replied, holding the phone to her ear.

"Send them in," he instructed.

"Hi, Mayor Crinkle," said Mr. and Mrs. Lyte as they all went into his office.

Lyla gave the mayor a wave.

"The place hasn't changed a bit, except for your new secretary," Mr. Lyte commented.

Mayor Crinkle came from behind his chair and shook Mr. Lyte's hand. "When you left I needed a new camera person, so Ms. Weatherspoon took your old job, and I hired my new secretary just before I went out of town," he explained. "And good morning to you Mrs. Lyte and Lyla."

"So how was the convention," Lyla asked.

"Very informative," he answered. "So what brings you all to City Hall today?"

Mr. Lyte looked at his daughter and said, "Lyla has something to share with you."

"You know your dumpsite east of Program Park?" Lyla began.

"Yes," said Mayor Crinkle.

Lyla went on, "My friends and I went there the other day…"

"That place is *not* safe for kids," Mayor

Crinkle interrupted, looking at Lyla with disappointed eyes.

"That's what I keep on telling her," Mrs. Lyte said, putting her hands on her hips.

"Well," Lyla paused, then went on, "we grew a Loot Tree."

Mayor Crinkle was confused by the name. "You grew what type of tree?" he asked.

Mr. Lyte butted in and spoke for Lyla. "That's their secret name for money," he explained.

"You know like, cash, dough, moolah," Lyla added. "In Spanish they call it dinero."

Her mom nudged her. "I think he gets it now," she whispered.

Mayor Crinkle's face lit up. "You grew a money tree in the dumpsite," he bellowed.

"They sure did," Mr. Lyte said, nodding his head.

"I have to take a seat," Mayor Crinkle said, going back to his chair.

"Are you OK?" Mrs. Lyte asked. She was a little worried that the mayor was going to pass out.

"She has more to tell you," Mr. Lyte told the mayor.

"There's more?" asked a frazzled mayor.

"Wait!" he said. He picked up the phone and called Ms. McGee. "Can you please bring me a cup of water?"

"OK, sir." Within seconds she came in with a paper cup of cold water. The mayor gulped it down. "OK, you can continue," he said to Lyla.

Lyla started back up. "Mrs. Holmes found out about the money tree and has been taking the money and is going to pay people to vote for her."

"So that's how she's funding her campaign," Mayor Crinkle exclaimed. "The snake!" he said grinding his teeth.

"Can she buy people's votes?" asked Mr. Lyte.

"I think it's *illegal* to buy votes," the mayor answered. "But let me check with my attorney, Laura Shields. If anyone should know she should."

The mayor picked up the phone and made the call.

Lyla looked at the mayor with worried eyes as

he hung up. "What did she say?"

"She said she needs to do a little research," replied Mayor Crinkle. "And will let me know tomorrow."

Suddenly, everyone was startled by the wailing sound of a police siren followed by a loud voice speaking through a megaphone.

They all dashed out of the building to see what was going on.

It was a procession, with Officer Gilbert's police car leading the way, its lights flashing. Trailing closely behind, Mrs. Holmes was sticking her long neck out of the window of her Beetle yelling through a megaphone, "I'm giving five dollars for your vote!"

Both cars stopped right in front of City Hall.

Mayor Crinkle yelled, attempting to drown out the megaphone, "Stop with that loud squealing!"

"You *can't* stop me from campaigning," Mrs. Holmes yelled back, speaking even more loudly into the megaphone to annoy the mayor.

As Officer Gilbert got out of his car, Mayor

Crinkle said to him, "I can't believe you are part of this mayhem."

"As Coverfield's police, I have a responsibility to help everyone," Officer Gilbert replied. "And that's what I'm doing, sir. Making sure drivers on the road will clear the way to avoid any accidents."

"Helping to disturb the peace," Mayor Crinkle said sarcastically, shaking his head in disgust.

Officer Gilbert responded, "Call it what you want, sir. I'm only doing my job."

"There is a place and time for this," Mayor Crinkle said. "And this is definitely neither."

"Those sound like debating words to me," Mrs. Holmes said. "I challenge *you* to a debate!"

All eyes were on Mayor Crinkle to see if he would accept the challenge.

Lyla said in a low voice, "Don't be scared Mayor Crinkle,"

Her encouraging words helped. He eyeballed Mrs. Holmes. "If that's what you want," he said. "When?"

"Tomorrow at Program Park!" Mrs. Holmes said.

With a burst of confidence Mayor Crinkle responded, "I accept!"

15

The Debate

The mayoral debate was shown on every tubevision in Coverfield. The whole town was talking about it. The park was packed to capacity with eager townspeople ready to listen to both candidates. Mr. Holmes crafted a makeshift stage and set up two podiums with separate microphones. There were folding chairs placed out for the audience.

Lyla and her parents attended along with the other Troops and their families. This time they made sure to sit in the front of the audience. Because Ms. Verdak had her class conduct a debate as a social studies project, she was asked to be the moderator.

A smiling Ms. Verdak came onto the stage and took a microphone off a stand. "Good afternoon, people of Coverfield!"

"Good afternoon," the audience replied.

"Thank you for attending the first ever mayoral debate in Coverfield," said Ms. Verdak, walking across the stage.

"Woo hoo!" the audience cheered.

Ms. Verdak went on, "I will now introduce the candidates. The first one is our very own mayor...Mayor Charles Crinkle."

Mayor Crinkle walked on to the stage and waved to the crowd. Then he took his place behind the podium to the right.

His biggest supporters were the Troops. "Have no mercy on Mrs. Holmes!" Nick shouted, cupping his hands and screaming between them.

"Let's go, Mayor Crinkle!" Lyla hollered.

Samantha held up three fingers. "Give her your best to the third power!" she yelled.

"Really, do you always have to use math terms?" Nick asked, shaking his head.

"We *love* you, Mayor Crinkle!" Megan and

Mary screamed, clasping each other's hands and raising them in a shape of a pyramid.

"Our second candidate is Mrs. Patricia Holmes," Ms. Verdak said, standing to the side and allowing the audience to have a full view of Mrs. Holmes. She came out, giddy with excitement, flinging money onto the stage.

The crowd erupted and started roaring, "Mrs. Holmes for mayor!"

Mayor Crinkle was instantly worried. *They love her already*, he thought.

After hyping up the crowd, Mrs. Holmes took a series of bows and went behind her podium.

Ms. Verdak began the debate. "My first question to the candidates is, What impact will you have as the mayor of Coverfield?" She pointed to Mayor Crinkle, indicating that he should answer first.

"Ahem," the mayor cleared his throat. "As mayor, I will continue to create a better life for the people of Coverfield, by creating new businesses, new jobs, and better educational opportunities for our children. Coverfield will always be a great place to live. I will always keep our streets safe, the parks clean, the school updated, and City Hall in tip-top shape."

Lyla and the Troops' smiles were as bright as the sun that beamed down on the audience. The crowd clapped.

"That's baloney," Mrs. Holmes murmured, sneering at Mayor Crinkle.

Then Ms. Verdak faced Mrs. Holmes and said, "The same question goes to you, Candidate Two."

"It's all about the money," declared Mrs.

Holmes, arrogantly. "I will provide a better life for the people of Coverfield by putting money in their pockets."

The audience was ecstatic. Mr. Holmes gestured to the crowd to cheer more loudly, and they did.

"If you're tired of being broke, raise your hand," Mrs. Holmes said, raising her hand first and holding up five-dollar bills.

The majority of hands flew up.

"Make some noise if you want to take home Abraham Lincoln on election day," she told the audience.

The cheering became earsplitting.

Ms. Verdak took control of the crowd as if they were her students. "OK, quiet down!" she said. The audience simmered down and she went on. "My second question for the candidates is, Will you increase or decrease the taxes if you win the election?"

This time Mrs. Holmes was the first to answer. "I'm about putting money in your hands...not taking money out," she said firmly.

"Vote for me and I'll do away with taxes forever."

What she said hit the audience like a ton of bricks. They were stunned at first, because they had never heard such a thing. "Did I hear correctly?" asked an audience member.

"You sure did," another said. "*No more* taxes. Great! I hate paying sales tax on groceries."

"Awesome!" the first said, beaming. "Because I've owed property taxes for the last ten years."

Nearly everyone rooted for Mrs. Holmes. Those that were for Mayor Crinkle began to flip sides.

"Mayor Crinkle, it's your turn to answer the question." Ms. Verdak got his attention.

Mayor Crinkle threw a slew of questions at the audience. "How are we going to fix our streets? How are we going to improve our schools? How are we going to pay our teachers and Coverfield's police? How are we going to keep Coverfield's hospital open?"

"If the citizens of Coverfield weren't so sick of taxes," interrupted Mrs. Holmes, sticking her finger in her throat and pretending to throw up.

"They wouldn't have to go to the hospital."

"I'm sick of your empty promises," Mayor Crinkle said, pointing at her angrily.

Ms. Verdak stepped in before it got out of hand and pleaded, "Mrs. Holmes, please allow the other candidate to finish his response."

The mayor continued, "We *can't* get rid of taxes. Each year I make the best decision possible in raising or lowering taxes. And as mayor I will continue do the same thing."

The audience booed.

"Magnificent job, Candidates," Ms. Verdak said. Then she strolled to the front of the stage. "Now, the audience will have an opportunity to ask the questions," she said, pointing to the microphone stand in front of the stage. "One at a time, please approach the microphone and ask your question."

The first person to approach the microphone was Mr. Johnson, president of the ELUA. He couldn't reach the microphone, so Ms. Verdak hurried off stage and lowered the stand.

A frustrated Mr. Johnson was short, direct,

and to the point, "As mayor, what are you going to do with those blasted books piling up on the vacant land?" Even though the question was directed to both candidates, he stared at Mayor Crinkle as he asked it.

"As I told you before, sir, I'm trying to raise loot...I mean money...to build a new library!" Mayor Crinkle responded with a note of annoyance in his voice.

"So how much money have you raised up to today?" Mr. Johnson asked, continuing to bash the mayor.

"None," Mayor Crinkle answered, avoiding speaking into the microphone.

Mr. Johnson had a *got you* look on his face. "I didn't hear you," he said cupping his hand around his left ear.

The mayor projected his voice into the microphone and said, "I haven't raised any money so far." It was clear that he was embarrassed.

"Ohhh!" the crowd said.

"Well, maybe we need a new mayor who can be more monetarily effective," Mr. Johnson commented, grinning.

"Is it my turn to answer the question?" Mrs. Holmes asked.

"Yes," said Ms. Verdak.

"I have more than enough money to build the library," Mrs. Holmes said, boastfully, looking directly at Mr. Johnson. "But I'm not building a useless library."

"We knew it," the Troops said together. "Booo, booo!" they all began to call out.

Mrs. Holmes took out a lighter from her pocket and flicked it. "As mayor, my first task will be to *burn* that pile of books to a crisp."

Lyla couldn't take it anymore. She could no longer sit in the audience and not voice her opinion. "You stole from us," she yelled, standing on her chair.

"Who said that?" Mrs. Holmes asked, searching the crowd to put a face to the public accusation. "Who are you to accuse me?"

"Her name is Lyla, and I'm her mom, Mrs. Lyte!" Mrs. Lyte announced, standing up for her daughter.

"And I'm her dad," Mr. Lyte added, proudly.

Mrs. Holmes was fuming with anger. "Your little misfit should not go around making false accusations," she said.

The other Troops stood, and with one accord they said, "Lyla's right."

"You bamboozled us," Megan bellowed.

"That means tricked." Nick turned around and defined the word for the crowd. "And she promised us a pizza party," he added.

"The Loot Tree does not belong to you all," Mrs. Holmes said.

16

Stampede

"We grew the Loot Tree," Lyla said, pointing at Mrs. Homes.

The audience was baffled by Lyla's statement and began whispering, "What's a Loot Tree?"

"I found that money on my own." Mrs. Holmes stayed calm as she disputed Lyla's claim.

The whispering grew into conversations among the audience. "It's a money tree! They grew money. Those are the same kids that grew books."

"You found it with our help," Mary yelled.

"You would have never known where it was if you hadn't duped us," Lyla went on.

Nick stood and faced the crowd. "Dupe also means trick."

"Sit down!" said the Troops to Nick.

"Geez, take a chill pill. I was only making sure they knew what it meant," Nick said, sliding back into his seat.

"Ha, ha, ha!" laughed Mrs. Holmes. "I simply asked and you little people told me where it was at. Don't be mad at me, be mad at yourselves."

"So why did you have to dress up like our principal," Samantha asked.

"I was trying out my new costume for Halloween," said Mrs. Holmes, guiltless.

Lyla jumped back in and said, "We are all tired of your trickery and we will not let you win the election with *our* Loot Tree."

"What's in the dumpsite is mine," Mrs. Holmes declared. Caught up in the moment, Mrs. Holmes didn't realize she had just advertised the location of the Loot Tree.

"The Loot Tree is in the dumpsite," the crowd repeated. It was a stampede as the crowd quickly began to disperse. Some jumped into their cars, and some just ran to the dumpsite. It was absolutely chaotic.

Samantha bellowed at Mrs. Holmes. "See what you did! Now everyone knows about the Loot Tree!"

"Oops!" she said. "Come on, Henry Holmes, let's get to that dumpsite." She led her husband by the hand.

Lyla was worried, "Dad we have to get to that dump site too," she said.

"Let's go everyone," Mr. Lyte said, leading the way. They jumped into the family van and rushed off with the other Troops and their families.

"Mr. Butler, to the limo," Mayor Crinkle directed, walking briskly to his car.

When they arrived at the dumpsite, there was a long line of townspeople waiting for their turn to get their share of the money.

They all jumped out of their vehicles and maneuvered through the line. "Excuse me, excuse me," Mr. Lyte said, as he bumped into people.

When they reached the front, Mrs. Holmes was plucking five-dollar bills from the Loot Tree and handing them one by one to people, while Mr. Holmes was reminding them to vote for his wife.

"Thank you, and remember election day is two weeks away," announced Mrs. Holmes.

Lyla told Mrs. Holmes to stop. Her voice caught everyone's attention. "Leave the money on the Loot Tree," she demanded. "That money is for building the new library."

Mrs. Holmes looked at Lyla, pointed to the ground, and said, "Unlike that tree in your backyard filled with books, the money tree grew on city property. So, if we, the citizens of Coverfield, don't want to build a stinking library with the money, it *can't* happen!"

Lyla turned to Mayor Crinkle, who had just arrived. "Mayor Crinkle owns the dumpsite," she said.

"Wrong! Little Ms. Know-it-all...who knows nothing!" Mrs. Holmes said in a malicious tone. "This dumpsite is owned by the City of Coverfield."

By this time all of the Troops were staring at Mayor Crinkle as their savior. "Tell her she's wrong," Samantha cried.

"Yeah, so she can give us back our money," Mary added.

"I'm sorry kids," Mayor Crinkle said with a disappointed voice. "I do not own this dumpsite. It's city property."

The Troops' faces fell. They couldn't believe Mayor Crinkle's response. Mrs. Holmes stood there grinning with a look that said "I told you so" and destroyed their hopes of ever building a new library. "If you little people would have listened, we could have avoided all of this unnecessary drama," she said.

So it's up to the majority of townspeople to decide what to do with the money that grew on the tree," Mayor Crinkle went on, sadly.

Mrs. Holmes walked in front of the crowd. "Raise your hands if you want the money to go to you...and you...and you!" She pointed to people in the crowd.

A sea of hands rose high in the air. Some folks even raised two hands. The crowd chanted "Money, money, money!"

"So go get your loot!" Mrs. Holmes shouted, mocking the Troops.

"Wait!" yelled Mrs. Shields, bursting through the crowd. She was dressed in a tan business skirt suit.

"And who are you?" Mrs. Holmes asked.

"I'm Mayor Crinkle's attorney," Mrs. Shields replied. "And I assume you are Mrs. Patricia Holmes—the other candidate in the electoral race."

"Yes!" Mrs. Holmes replied. "If you are here to collect your five dollars for voting for me, you have to go to the back of the line."

The crowd shouted, "Yeah, we were here first!"

"I'm not here to get money for voting for you," Mrs. Shields said, offended. "That's called *vote buying* and it's illegal in the United States."

The news hushed the crowd. The mayor and the Troops were smiling from ear to ear.

Mrs. Shields went on, "And if you do choose to pay people to vote for you, you will go to jail and will receive a fine as well."

Mrs. Holmes was shocked, but within seconds she got over it. "It doesn't matter. I didn't want to be mayor of this town anyway. That money still belongs to the people of this town. I said go get your money!" she repeated, pointing back and forth from the crowd to the tree.

Instinctively, the Troops ran and stood between the Loot Tree and the money-hungry crowd, locking hands.

Mr. Lyte jumped in front of the crowd and

urged them to think twice, "They're only children. What if these were your kids?"

The crown stood still.

"Well, I don't have kids," said Mrs. Holmes. "And I'm not going let a bunch of little muskrats stop me from getting that money."

Without a word, the Troops tightened up their grips.

Mrs. Holmes took off toward the human barricade. With every move she made to get by, the Troops moved, blocking her, and she became more and more frazzled.

After a few frustrating attempts, Mrs. Holmes stopped.

"What is more important, helping Coverfield or helping yourselves?" Lyla asked, addressing the crowd. "My dad was kinda wrong when he said money is the root of all evil. Its people's intentions that are evil. All we wanted to do was grow money to help the town, but all of you want to use the money for yourselves."

The crowd began to ponder Lyla's words.

"Don't listen to this little girl!" Mrs. Holmes said, turning to face the crowd. "You all need this money just as bad as me."

A leaf fell from the tree and drifted on to Nick's Mohawk, causing him to turn his head around.

"The children of Coverfield need a library," Lyla said. "Don't you all remember when you used to be able to go to the library and pick any book and get *lost* in reading?"

"Those times are over!" Mrs. Holmes yelled.

Nick began whispering to get Lyla's attention.

"Lyla, look over there."

She cocked her head slightly to the left and whispered back, "Can't you see I'm giving my speech."

"But look," Nick said, nodding his head in the direction of the tree.

Mrs. Holmes cried, "Money makes us happy, not a book."

Lyla pleaded with the crowd. "Please, I ask all of you. Don't listen to her. You all are better than that."

"Are you going to just stand there and listen to a little girl who doesn't even pay bills? Who never knew how it feels to be broke?" Mrs. Holmes said, trying hard to convince the crowd.

"Lyla," Nick whispered louder.

"What?" asked Lyla, a bit annoyed.

"The tree," Nick said. He unlocked his hands and turned to fully faced the Loot Tree.

Meagan, Samantha, and Mary turned around before Lyla, and they too were thrown aback at what they saw. "Something is happening," they said.

"And it's *not* good," Nick added.

Lyla finally turned around and saw that the lush green leaves of the tree were turning dark brown. "Oh, no!" she cried. "What's happening?"

One by one all of the money began to fall off of the tree followed by dead brown leaves.

Mrs. Holmes saw the faces in the crowd look shocked and turned around. She immediately ran toward the tree and cradled her arms, basket-like, trying to catch the falling money. "Somebody save this tree," bawled Mrs. Holmes. "I need the money."

"The tree can't survive in this polluted environment," Mrs. Lyte said. "There's no fresh water and not enough sun light."

As they watched, the tree withered and died.

Tears filled Lyla's eyes. "What are we going to do now?" she asked

"Look at all of you," said Mayor Crinkle, finally speaking up. "I used to be just like some of you, greedy and selfish, until this little girl showed me how to be a better person. We should be proud that our children want a library to read books."

Mrs. Holmes stood up. "It's all your fault!" she said, pointing at Lyla. "Wait till I get my hands on you!"

As she lunged at Lyla, Mr. Holmes stuck out his leg, causing his wife to trip and fall right on her face in a pool of green goop. "That's enough, Patricia," he said, looking down at his wife. "The Loot Tree is gone."

"I guess the new library wasn't meant to be," Lyla said to the Troops.

Mr. Johnson walked up and said, "Life should be about helping *each* other." He reached into his pocket, pulled out a crisp five-dollar bill and handed it to Lyla. "I want to make a donation to the new Coverfield library."

The Troops were shocked as they looked at the five-dollar bill Lyla held in her hand.

Mr. Johnson started a chain reaction. "Me too," said Mrs. Shields. *Everyone* in the crowd began pulling out money and passing it forward to the front. Some were even writing checks.

The Troops jumped up and down, thrilled.

There was lots of hugging.

With Dentapotomus in hand, Lyla's mom looked down and said, "After today, you are never to come back to this dumpsite."

"You don't have to worry about that," Lyla said, wrapping her arms around her mom.

"Give me five," Dentapotomus said.

"Oh, no!" Lyla exclaimed. "My little brother is money hungry too."

But then she saw he was holding up his hand, palm outward. "Clap," he said.

Lyla and her mom laughed as Lyla gave him a high five.

She turned to her dad and said, "It worked out after all."

"Sometimes, it rains before the sunshine," Mr. Lyte said.

"But it didn't rain today," Lyla replied, confused. "Oh, I get it, another one of your quotes."

They looked at each other and smiled.

Lyla Lyte and the Loot Tree

Don't forget to read about Lyla's first adventure...

★ "[A] fast-paced and well-written novel. An impressive story about a girl whose courage transforms a town."
— *Kirkus Reviews* (starred review)

215

CPSIA information can be obtained
at www.ICGtesting.com
Printed in the USA
FFOW01n1835270316
22705FF